## Once she'd decided that she wanted him, she hadn't stopped to consider...

Did he...not want this? Nina could address the matter in a straightforward way. Yet she opted to play coy instead. Because that always worked. "Hey," she said, taking a step forward. "We have a few things to celebrate tonight. Let's order champagne."

"Did you want me to kiss you in there?"

Oh, God! Why couldn't he let her play coy? "Yeah... about that... Did you not want to?"

"I had to be sure," he said. "You remember saying you didn't want to sleep with me, right?"

"When did I say that?"

"The first night we slept together—or shared a bed, I should say. I don't want to be something you regret."

"That's not possible."

\* \* \*

*Scandal in the VIP Suite* by Nadine Gonzalez is part of the Miami Famous series.

D0052115

Dear Reader,

Fans of glamour, drama and modern love conundrums, welcome to the party!

*Scandal in the VIP Suite* is the first of (hopefully) many Miami Famous stand-alone romances, filled with Caribbean and Latinx characters freely pursuing love and happiness, yet always teetering on the edge of scandal. I promise to make my heroes and heroines larger-than-life but involve them in truthfully tender relationships.

My debut for Harlequin Desire is set in Miami Beach's famed Ocean Drive. You'll meet Julian Knight, a beleaguered action movie star whose masculine image has become toxic to his career. Nina Taylor is a bestselling author suffering from writer's block. When Nina and Julian get past their initial reservations, they find they are the perfect fit, creatively and emotionally. I hope you love them as much as I do.

For more about my upcoming releases, visit www.nadine-gonzalez.com and follow on Instagram and Twitter, @_nadinegonzalez. Need more Miami modern love? Check out the Miami Dreams series with Harlequin Kimani Romance.

Until the next one!

*Nadine*

# NADINE GONZALEZ

———

# SCANDAL IN THE VIP SUITE

# HARLEQUIN
# DESIRE

Recycling programs
for this product may
not exist in your area.

ISBN-13: 978-1-335-23268-7

Scandal in the VIP Suite

Copyright © 2021 by Nadine Seide

This edition published by arrangement with Harlequin Books S.A.

For questions and comments about the quality of this book,
please contact us at CustomerService@Harlequin.com.

Harlequin Enterprises ULC
22 Adelaide St. West, 40th Floor
Toronto, Ontario M5H 4E3, Canada
www.Harlequin.com

**Printed in U.S.A.**

**Nadine Gonzalez** is the daughter of Haitian immigrants, born in New York City. She was raised both in New York and Port-au-Prince, Haiti. A lawyer by profession, she lives in Miami, Florida, and shares her home with her Cuban American husband and their beautiful son.

Nadine writes joyous contemporary romance featuring a diverse cast of characters, American, Caribbean and Latinx. She networks on Twitter but lives on Instagram! Check out @_nadinegonzalez.

For more information, visit her website, nadine-gonzalez.com.

### Books by Nadine Gonzalez

### Harlequin Desire

#### *Miami Famous*

*Scandal in the VIP Suite*

### Harlequin Kimani Romance

*Exclusively Yours*
*Unconditionally Mine*

Visit her Author Profile page at Harlequin.com, or nadine-gonzalez.com, for more titles.

You can also find Nadine Gonzalez on Facebook, along with other Harlequin Desire authors, at Facebook.com/harlequindesireauthors.

Sincere thanks to my editor, Errin Toma. It has been a pleasure working with you. Here's to a long, productive relationship!

Shout-out to Roxanna Elden, best writing buddy, and the Miami Book Fair and Writers Institute for their unwavering support.

With regards to craft, I would first like to thank my husband, Ariel. You are always my first story editor. Special thanks to my sister Martine for the unlimited brainstorming sessions that resulted in the perfect meet-cute. To my "creative consultants," Ian Midgley and Julia Taylor, you have breathed life into my first Jamaican British hero.

To my sisters Martine and Murielle: your support means everything to me.

A special shout-out to TEAM 12! You are the best #bookstagram helpers a budding author could have.

Finally to Ariel and Nathaniel, let's dream on!

# One

It seemed to Nina Taylor that she'd been traveling forever. Her flight was delayed at JFK, and the plane had spent an eternity in the queue at Miami International Airport before reaching its gate. Outside, she slipped on dark sunglasses to block out Miami's Technicolor brightness and settled into the back of a cab. It was unreasonably hot—even for July—and the fake leather seat stuck to her bare arms. The driver loaded her bags into the trunk and slipped behind the wheel. "Where to?"

"Fifteen ten Ocean Drive."

"Sand Castle? Good choice." He adjusted the rearview mirror. "What brings you to Miami?"

A simple enough question. Most people wouldn't have to lie. "Meeting a friend."

"Nice! Nice!" The driver nodded. A bald spot on the back of his head revealed a patch of shiny brown skin.

He eased into traffic. "I tell my grandkids to have fun! Take chances! Enjoy their youth!"

"Sounds like you're a good grandpa."

He glanced at her in the rearview mirror. "You look like my granddaughter. Which island are you from?"

The question didn't surprise Nina. People from the islands had a sixth sense for this stuff. But Nina's Caribbean roots were so deeply buried, Manhattan was the only island she could legitimately claim as her own. Just then, a massive SUV sped past them, cutting them off. A honking match ensued. The driver returned his attention to the road, saving her from having to answer his question. It was better this way; her family tree was more of a twisted, brittle vine.

As the AC kicked in, Nina got comfortable. This was not her first trip to Miami, but the memory of the last trip was blurred in a Jell-O shot glaze. She was twenty-three at the time and on assignment for *Belle*, a women's magazine. She was thirty-one now, and her taste in cocktails had greatly evolved.

Nina lost herself in the view. Miami was one big, bloated suburb. One strip of highway connected to the next with a few well-placed palm trees to maintain the illusion of paradise. Soon enough they reached a causeway soaring above the dazzling bay, and everything changed. Suburban sprawl gave way to waterfront mansions and glass condo towers. Traffic was at a crawl when they inched past the iconic Welcome to Miami Beach sign. Nina snapped a photo with her phone, excitement bubbling inside her. By the time they veered onto Ocean Drive and pulled up to the hotel's glossy black gates, Nina's outlook on life shifted. Maybe this solo trip wasn't the worst idea she'd ever had.

The mansion-turned-private boutique hotel stood proud in the sun. It had all the trappings of classic Mediterranean style: chalk-white walls and an angled terracotta tile roof, randomly placed windows—some arched, some not—and French doors opening to Juliet balconies. But it wasn't until she entered the courtyard that Nina hit all-time Zen. The villa soared three stories above an interior garden complete with a fountain, each floor opening onto balconies with iron rails as fine as lace.

*Mom would have loved this.* The thought escaped her like a leaf caught in a breeze. But it assured her that she was in the right place.

Nina approached the front desk, gave her information and helped herself to a complimentary mint.

"I'm sorry, Ms. Taylor. There's an issue with your reservation."

The words no weary traveler ever wanted to hear.

"What's the issue?" Nina asked. "I booked my stay a month ago."

"Not sure. The manager will tell you more."

The clerk offered her a mini-bottle of water, but Nina would not be placated. The sharp click-clack of high heels on tile announced the arrival of the manager. Nina readied herself for a fight.

"Welcome to Sand Castle, Ms. Taylor! I'm the general manager, Grace Guzman."

Despite the circumstances, Nina winced at the hotel's generic name. It wasn't suited to a Mediterranean-style mansion, and Nina had half a mind to let this Guzman woman know.

"Come with me. Let's get you sorted."

Nina followed the manager along a cloistered walkway to a small office that might have been a butler's pantry in another era. A nameplate read simply, "Graciela Guzman." The stark white walls were cluttered with charcoal sketches framed in gold. She sat behind a desk that was free of all clutter and got down to it. "Ms. Taylor, the suite you requested is no longer available."

Nina dropped into an empty chair and stared at her. "I don't understand. I booked the Oasis spa getaway package one month ago."

"Sand Castle has no official spa suite," Grace said. "All our rooms are suited for relaxing stays."

"Not according to your website."

The spa package had included the two-bedroom top-floor suite. Jackie Onassis had called it an oasis when she'd spent a night in February 1988 and the name had stuck. *Belle* magazine had ranked it among the top ten hotels for the sophisticated traveler—a list that Nina had curated without ever stepping foot on any of the listed properties. It was her late mother's dream to spend the night there. Nina was here to fulfill that dream. If that weren't the case, Nina would have picked a less expensive, less pretentious hotel. Even as the thought crossed her mind, she knew it wasn't true. The instant her cab pulled up to the gates and her luggage had exchanged hands, she had succumbed to the old mansion's charm.

"Ms. Taylor, try to understand. The Oasis is our equivalent of the presidential suite. It's subject to availability."

"Is the president coming?" Nina asked. "Because according to CNN, he's expected to give a speech in Johannesburg."

Grace's eyes narrowed. "We've had to make it available for an important guest. It's all last-minute, and I apologize. Since you're traveling alone, would you settle for a superior room instead?"

What? She wasn't going to settle for some single-lady-traveler downgrade! "I'd mind very much."

Grace smiled coolly. Nina noted the lovely creases at the corners of her eyes. In her midfifties or so, she was a beauty and knew it. Her foundation makeup didn't blend well into her olive complexion, but otherwise she was perfect. Wearing a belted yellow dress and heels, Grace had the advantage of style. Nina felt plain by comparison in her go-to travel uniform: T-shirt, skinny jeans, don't-mess-with-me shades and ballerina flats.

Prepping for this trip, Nina had scrubbed, peeled and waxed. On the plane, she'd slathered serum on her face; as a result, her matte brown skin was dewy, but not in a good way. Her hair hung in a limp braid down her back. And now it was clear that in her zealous preparation for her Miami getaway, she'd neglected all the smaller moments leading to it, like arriving in style at a luxury hotel, dressed to kill and prepared to confront the arrogant staff.

Grace checked her gold watch. "Your stay is important to us, I assure you."

Nina's anger spiked. "Not as important as this person you've given my suite to!"

It was probably a lost cause, but there was no way she was going to make this easy on management.

"We think you'll be happy in our Garden Room."

Nina shut her eyes. A tingling sensation spread from her chest to her throat, a sign that things were going to get loud and ugly. She thought it best to warn the other woman. "I'm sorry, but I'm about to throw a fit."

The flutter of Grace's unnaturally thick lashes was

the only hint that Nina had gotten under her skin. "Naturally, your account will reflect the change in price."

Nina remained stone-faced. Grace tried a different tactic. "What if we offered a complimentary in-room massage? Would that make up for the inconvenience?"

"No, it wouldn't." She was so brittle with exhaustion, if anyone laid a hand on her, she'd snap like a twig.

"How about an extra night's stay on us?" Grace proposed.

That would round up her trip to seven nights. But why stop there? "Make it two nights."

Grace made a show of checking her computer before tossing her reading glasses onto the glass desktop. "That'll work."

Nina nodded. She was disappointed, to be sure. The point of this trip was to honor her mother with the sort of Jackie O experience she'd deserved, but even the most unhinged traveler had to yield to reason. The Garden Room would do for now.

Grace pressed an intercom buzzer and called for a porter. Rising from behind her desk, she said, "Let's get you settled."

Nina followed Grace out the office just in time to witness the commotion in the courtyard marking the arrival of new guests. Grace promptly abandoned her and, in a state of agitation that didn't suit her, went off to greet the newcomers. A hostess trailed behind her with a tray of champagne flutes. Nina wondered where the welcome committee had been when she'd arrived only moments earlier. Then it dawned on her—she'd been booted out of the Oasis to accommodate the excessively attractive people making their entrance.

A power couple if she'd ever seen one. The man

was stunning. Nina hated to admit it, but there was no tap-dancing around the obvious. Tall, broad and with a profile that matched the marble busts hidden in the mansion's many alcoves, he was hard to ignore. His complexion was raw honey, taking on a golden patina in the sun. His eyes were concealed behind smoky glasses, and he wore his long, wavy hair tied neatly at the nape of his neck. Given three guesses, Nina would go with soccer player, baseball star or prizefighter—middleweight division. He looked important, even though his appearance was somewhat disheveled in a black blazer worn over a wrinkled white T-shirt paired with faded jeans. The woman was obviously younger, still in her twenties, but that was how those things sorted themselves out. She was blonde and wore the equivalent of Nina's travel uniform, elevated by a pair of black pumps. Nina imagined the couple getting settled in *her* suite, sipping champagne on *her* balcony before having sex on *her* custom double king bed—the absolute best sex in the world. That image alone prompted her to move all her resentment from Grace Guzman to the power couple with a simple mental balance transfer.

Nina hid behind a pillar and watched as Grace, clumsy with giddiness, gushed over the couple. The man laughed at something she said, the full, throaty laugh of a man who had everything going for him. Something about it sent a ripple down Nina's spine.

A porter approached, startling her. "Ms. Taylor, my name is Jim. Please come this way."

She followed him up a grand, winding staircase, that unnerving laugh licking at her ears. And because she couldn't let a damn thing go, Nina tossed a final look over her shoulder. To her surprise, Mr. VIP was at the bottom of the stairs staring up at her without the filter of the smoky sunglasses. Mortified, she held his gaze a beat longer than necessary for no other reason than to prove that she wasn't. Their eyes locked, and for a split second it was just the two of them in the courtyard. Nina grabbed the handrail for support. Jim the porter called out, "This way, Ms. Taylor." Good thing, too, because for a moment there, she'd forgotten who she was and where she was headed.

On the second-floor landing, Jim turned to her. "Sorry about the commotion. You know how it is when Holly-wood comes calling."

Nina knew something about that. The daughter of a Broadway actress, she'd witnessed firsthand the frenzy the arrival of a Hollywood player could provoke. Her mother's friends would enjoy a collective orgasm when-ever a film actor signed up for a play. So...Hollywood? She'd been wrong on all three guesses.

"I shouldn't say this, but it's a madhouse down there. Glad my shift is over." Jim stopped abruptly and checked the key in his hand. "You're in Oasis? Really? I thought..."

"What?" Nina skipped a step and nearly tripped.

"We could have taken the private elevator," Jim said glumly. "Sorry about that."

"Uh...no worries. I could use the exercise."

"All right. Only one more flight to go."

The stairs wound up to the third floor. Nina looked over the rail down at the courtyard. The VIP couple was still chatting with Grace. She had time. To do what exactly? As she tried to puzzle that out, her gaze lin-gered on *him*. She had the luxury of staring at him un-challenged and took full advantage. An athlete would have had rough, rugged edges, but he was Hollywood beautiful: solid, symmetrical, smooth. His casual clothes looked expensive, and he wore them with effortless cool. His smile was like the sun. Nina's core turned to jelly, and it had nothing to do with the languid heat.

"Ms. Taylor?"

*Damn it! Busted again!*

Nina swiveled around and followed Jim, her heart racing. On the third floor, potted lavender plants lined the way down a hall to a pair of carved mahogany doors. She was at the threshold of paradise, but what was the plan here? Take a quick look around. That was all. And why not? She'd been robbed of the experience.

Jim punched a code in the keypad and explained that a new code would be sent to her via email. Then he inserted a hefty skeleton key in the lock and turned it until the lock clicked. Sweat beaded at Nina's temples, and she wondered about the maximum sentence for trespassing. The door swung open to reveal a Greek key tiled floor that seemed to go on forever. Jim ushered her into a sitting room furnished with antiques. A crystal chandelier hung overhead, and French doors opened to a wide balcony. Nina's anxiety gave way to a rush of excitement.

Jim stacked her luggage on a loading table in the foyer. "Would you like a tour?"

"No, thanks. I'm beat."

"Very well. The master suite is to your left, and the guest room to your right. Each room has a private bath."

Nina tipped Jim handsomely to better send him on his way. She preferred not to get him mixed up in this. As soon as the door shut behind him, she wasted no time storming the master bedroom suite, only to stand frozen at the threshold.

*This* was the famous Oasis. The space glowed. Honey oak furniture, gold leaf accents and yellow silk drapes all helped to spread the sunlit luster. A mural of hand-painted flowers crawled up the walls. The bed was a sea of blue silk anchored by four wood posters—and it called out to Nina. She went over, sat at the edge, bounced a bit to test the mattress, then she spilled onto her back. "Oh, yes," she murmured, staring up at the ceiling. A fresco depicted angels floating on tufted clouds. They looked down at her knowingly.

She made a mental note for her journal: *Elegant, opulent and a little too much! I love it!*

Only one more box to tick: a selfie. For good measure.

Nina sat up, pulled her phone from her pocket, smoothed her hair, selected a photo filter, tilted her head, pursed her lips, grimaced, attempted a smile and—

"Does the bed feel just right, Goldilocks?"

The phone fell from her hand. The masculine voice had a blunt British accent. It punched her in the gut and left her winded. Nina folded forward, squeezed her eyes shut and prayed that the angels frolicking on the ceiling would do her a favor and summon the angel of death.

*God, please! I'd rather die than live through this. Amen.*

# Two

The first thing he noticed was a flock of birds flying past the bell tower at the end of the courtyard. Julian Leroy Knight, better known as JL Knight, felt that he could've been anywhere in the world—Mexico, Spain or Cuba, where a similar estate stood. He'd done his research. This mansion was an exact replica of a villa in Havana's elegant suburb of Miramar. The original currently housed an embassy.

Julian exchanged pleasantries with the property manager, declined a glass of champagne and left his assistant, Kat, to handle the details of his stay. He ventured deeper into the yard. A central fountain stood as tall as him and struggled to mute the street noise. Day or night, Ocean Drive was a party. He should know. At nineteen, he'd left his home in England seeking adventure in the United States. He'd stayed with a family friend in Miami for a week before making his way down to South Beach. For six months, he worked for Sand Castle as a valet attendant, and during that time he never stepped foot past the iconic black gates. Access to the "main house" was denied to low-level staff. Fast-forward to today, and they were throwing him a parade.

The fuss was a balm to his bruised ego. Julian wasn't the celebrity that he had been five years ago, when his action films dominated the box office. In Hollywood, the whiff of failure was poison gas, and it followed you everywhere. Add to that a very public breakup and the public outcry over the portrayal of women in his latest release, and Julian was practically persona non grata everywhere. Except here in Miami, which was nice.

A grand staircase curved up to the second floor. He wandered to it and tested the sturdiness of the oak handrail. He'd worked carpentry for a while and appreciated the craft. A woman was making her way up the stairs. Tall, slim, light on her feet, cocoa-brown skin, body beautifully packaged in a pair of fitted jeans. She wore her coffee-black hair in a long braid that snaked down her back. When she glanced over her shoulder, looking directly at him, her long lashes veiled her eyes. But nothing could shield him from that scorching glare.

Fair was fair. After all, she'd caught him staring. Ogling women wasn't a habit of his, and this wasn't the time to start. He'd been labeled the poster boy for toxic masculinity; he couldn't afford any slipups. Only nothing about this felt like a slip. It felt pointed and personal. She held his gaze, and Julian couldn't break away. He watched, fascinated, as her cheeks turned the shade of wine. Who knew how long they'd have stayed like this if a porter hadn't called out to her?

With an imperious flip of her braid, she continued her ascent, turned a corner and disappeared. Julian fought back the impulse to give chase. What was the matter with him? He was here on business.

In the end, it was Kat who saved him from himself. She linked her arm around his and dragged him away. "Come on! I'd like to see the pool before we head upstairs."

They made their way to an open veranda overlooking the pool below. The manager explained that a previous owner had purchased the neighboring lot just to make space for it. Julian had to admire the audacity of a man who thought, *Screw it! I'll knock down a house and put a pool in its place.* But once he saw it, he was on board.

The pool was the true oasis, not some stuffy bedroom filled with antiques. It stretched one hundred feet wide and was paved in thousands of tiny gold tiles. Each corner was punctuated by urns set high on pedestals. A fountain spit water down the middle, sending ripples along the crystal surface. Julian yearned to dive in, but for now he'd settle for a photograph. He pulled his Nikon out of a well-worn, well-loved travel bag.

"Look at it!" Kat exclaimed. "Julian, isn't it gorgeous?"

He adjusted the lens of the camera and raised it to his eye. "Gorgeous."

"Would you like a closer look?" Grace offered.

"No, this works."

Julian framed the shot in his mind. He pictured a woman in a bikini floating on her back, eyes closed against the sun, hair like a halo around her head. Act one, scene one. He snapped the photo and put away the camera.

"Our annual Independence Day pool party is the most exclusive on the beach," Grace said. "It starts tomorrow at four. We'll end the night with fireworks."

Julian relied on his acting skills to fake interest. "Sounds great."

Grace nodded, pleased. "Now I'll show you to your private elevator."

As he, Kat and the manager squeezed into a rickety lift that led straight to his floor, Julian wondered if he might run into the woman on the stairs again, if only to apologize.

The lift opened to a wide, sun-filled walkway leading to a pair of sturdy doors. Grace ushered them inside, all the while entertaining Kat with the highlights of the mansion's storied past. In her excitement, she missed the luggage stacked neatly in the entrance. The Louis Vuitton weekender bag and matching tote did not belong to him. He was not a fancy-luggage type of guy.

"Come see the view from the balcony," Grace said.

Kat followed Grace. Julian swiveled on his heel and took off in the opposite direction. The master bedroom was behind a pair of thick wood doors. He drifted over, quietly turned the heavy brass knob and peeked through the crack. There she was. Taking a selfie on the bed.

Shit. This was not the second encounter he'd hoped for. Now instead of apologizing, he'd have to call security.

He entered the room. "Does the bed feel just right, Goldilocks?"

At his words, she stiffened and dropped her phone. He took no joy in her reaction. He didn't like seeing her so defeated where earlier she'd been so defiant. *Come on. Where's that fighting spirit?* When she finally stood to confront him, her eyes were wild with panic. Julian tried to muster something stronger than amused annoyance but came up short. If it were up to him, he'd let her escape and pretend this incident never happened. This wouldn't be the first time a fan tried to sneak into his hotel room. He was blasé enough to shrug it off. But it wasn't up to him. She didn't know it, but the countdown had begun. Before too long—

"Ah!" Kat screamed in Julian's ear. "What's going on? How did she get in?"

The manager stormed the bedroom. "Ms. Taylor!"

The porter arrived with Julian's plain black logo-free luggage and offered to call security.

Julian stepped forward to cover Ms. Taylor from the incoming fire. She may be an intruder, but she was *his* intruder. But she stepped out of his shadow and addressed the room.

"Settle down," she said. "This is just one big misunderstanding."

Her voice was calm. Julian liked that.

"Someone get Jim up here!" Grace yelled.

"Leave Jim out of it," she said. "It was a mistake. Probably *your* mistake. I bet this suite is still under my name."

"Ms. Taylor, we have an agreement. This suite is not yours, and you know it."

"What agreement?" Julian asked, and Ms. Taylor got him up to speed.

"The agreement we reached after she kicked me out to accommodate you."

Julian turned to Grace. "Is that true?"

She went pale. He had his answer.

An assistant arrived, flanked by security guards and

trailed by poor Jim. The comedy of errors checked out. The suite was still reserved under Ms. Taylor's name. Jim was given the wrong key at the front desk. To complicate matters, the hotel had no vacancies.

The assistant clutched an iPad with a white-knuckled grip. "We're fully booked for the holiday."

"I thought the Garden Room was available," Grace said, her voice thin.

"Full, ma'am." An elderly guest had thrown out his back and couldn't be moved until his pain medications kicked in. "Our hands are tied."

Grace switched to Spanish to vent her frustration. Julian glanced at Kat. She was chewing on her bottom lip the way she did when she was anxious. All this turmoil over a hotel room was ridiculous to Julian. People liked to treat him as if he were a descendant of the royal family, but he'd stayed in hostels and motels that he'd like to forget. He'd slept in his car for a month when he first moved out to Los Angeles. He'd gladly give up the suite, but unfortunately, he needed the buffer the private floor provided.

"That's enough," Julian said. "Ms. Taylor and I will figure this out. We'll draw straws or something. Please wait outside."

"Julian, it's not your job to figure this out," Kat said.

"I agree, Mr. Knight," Grace said.

"Even so, I'd prefer you clear the room."

After he ushered the delegation out the door, Julian turned to the crafty Ms. Taylor. She stared at him with a vacant expression, and he worried that she might have suffered a stroke. "Hey! Are you okay?"

She uncurled an index finger and pointed at him. "You're JL Knight!"

*Here we go.*

Julian cupped the nape of his neck and rubbed out the kinks. He could speak up now or let the madness run its course. He decided to let it run.

She continued to launch accusations. "And you're *British*?"

"Jamaican and British," he specified. "Is that bad?"

"I don't know! Malcolm Brown was from the South Bronx."

For two seasons, Julian had played paramedic Malcolm Brown on *Riverside Rescue*, a long-running network police procedural. Very few people remembered his early work. "I've been in a few projects since then."

"I wouldn't know," she said. "I binge-watched *Riverside* last Christmas, and Malcolm was my favorite."

"Thank you," he said. "And sorry for this mix-up. My assistant handled the travel arrangements. Usually she'll call, drop my name and—"

"And people drop everything?"

"Something like that."

"Must be nice," she said.

"You know what? It is."

"Well, I handle my own business. You should try it sometime."

"Want it back?" he offered. "I'll go elsewhere."

Sand Castle was central to his presence in Miami, but he wouldn't have insisted on staying here had he known the suite was booked. There was no shortage of five-star hotels on the beach. And in retrospect, showing up in Miami on a holiday weekend was a stupid idea.

"Keep it," she said firmly. "The manager will poison my food if you walk out. You're too *important*."

"How about we share it? There's no reason you can't stay here until the Garden, Fountain or whatever opens up."

"You're wrong." She folded her arms over her chest. "There are about one hundred reasons. Top of the list—stranger danger."

"Never played that game. Sounds fun."

What was he doing flirting with the woman he'd caught taking a selfie on his bed? Talk about stranger danger.

"It would only be for a night, maybe two," he said. "This place is huge. We could go for days and not run into each other."

"There *is* a second bedroom with a private bath," she said, speaking more to herself than to him.

"Look how much you know," Julian said.

"I wrote a piece about this hotel long ago," she said. "Also, the porter told me."

"Good old Jim?"

She looked uneasy. "I hope I didn't get him fired."

"If it helps, I'll put in a good word," Julian said. "So, you're a writer?"

She raised her chin. "I am."

"What do you write?"

"Books," she said. "Well…I wrote one book, but there are several formats."

"Okay."

He must have hit a sore spot. She was suddenly less sure of herself, stumbling over her words. But she was no less beautiful. The light from the windows washed over her face, warming her bronze skin and adding specks of gold to her brown eyes. Julian itched to reach for his camera.

There was a double knock on the door. He moved away from it. "They're getting restless. Time to decide."

She let out a sigh. "Well, what about the blonde?"

Her question left him confused. "Which blonde?"

"The one you're traveling with," she said. "She won't want me around. Three is a crowd."

"Blondes are people with parents and pets and feelings. They're objectified enough without you piling on, Ms. Taylor."

She wrapped her arms around her waist as if to control the spread of a full-body laugh. "I apologize, Mr. Knight. Thanks for shining a light on the plight of the blondes."

"You're welcome," Julian said. "Her name is Katia Wells, and she's my assistant."

"The one who booked your travel?"

"The same." Kat was in Florida to attend a family reunion. She'd gladly abandoned her seat on a commercial airline to fly private with him. A car was waiting outside to take her to her grandparents' house in Boca Raton. "If we were together, do you think she'd be waiting on the other side of the door?"

"I don't know anything about you or how you live your life," she said. "Which brings us back to stranger danger."

"Yeah? Of the two of us, only one has demonstrated a disregard for social norms."

A triple knock rattled the door. Kat called out to him. "Julian! I can get you a suite at the Fontainebleau."

That was timely information. He liked having options.

"We could both leave," he suggested to Ms. Taylor.

"I'm sure there's more than one available room at the Fontainebleau."

"Or we could both stay."

They fell silent and, in that silence, they reached an agreement. Still, there were some wrinkles to iron out. "Are you traveling alone?" he asked. "You booked this entire suite for yourself, or are you expecting a full bachelorette party?"

"Did anyone question you for wanting a suite to yourself?"

"It's mainly for privacy reasons," he said. "Which brings me to my one caveat."

"Just one? I have a few."

"You're a writer," Julian said.

"And you're an actor."

"You can't write about me or anything that happens while you're here."

She eyed him with suspicion. "What do you think will happen?"

"Not much," he said with a shrug. "I'm going to dive into bed as soon as everyone clears out. What are your plans?"

For the first time ever, she relaxed. Her rigid posture loosened, and her arms fell to her side. "Same. I'm exhausted."

"All right, then."

He went to open the door, but she stopped him. "Wait! Why are you being so nice?"

"This is not about niceness," he said. "It's about fairness. If I hadn't showed up, you wouldn't be in this position."

"I got a good deal out of it," she said.

"Yeah? What's the deal?"

"Two free nights."

"Not bad."

"Right?"

Another loud, imperious knock, and the manager scolded him from the other side of the door. "Mr. Knight! This is not how we do things at Sand Castle. Let us handle it."

This summit had to end. Julian was seriously sleep-deprived and all that knocking was drilling into his skull. He turned to her for confirmation. "Are we doing this?"

"Sure," she said. "I'll stay until my room becomes available. And don't worry; I have no interest in writing about you. A, I don't find you that compelling. B, I'm only really qualified to write about myself."

"Not compelling?"

There were feature stories dedicated to the rise and fall of his career. A talentless hack to some, an action hero legend to others, but nothing if not compelling.

She rolled her eyes and murmured something about fragile Hollywood egos.

"Excuse me," he said.

"Open the door before they call the cops."

"Fair point." He'd sweep up the shards of his ego later. "Let's face the firing squad."

# Three

*Ha! Joke's on me! The second bedroom is actually a tidy study with an attached bath. All this opulence and I'm spending the night on a pullout couch.*

Nina put aside her journal and closed her eyes. She'd kept a diary since childhood. An only child, her diary was often the guardian of her deepest secrets. When her fiction had failed to sell, she'd turned a year's worth of old journals from her late teens into a memoir—a decision she now regretted. Regretting important life decisions was becoming a pattern.

She never should have come to Miami. What had she hoped to achieve? Closure? *I mean...come on!* This was life, not the Oprah show, and this trip was one big, unmitigated disaster.

Oh, but that wasn't entirely true. There was one tall, dark and handsome mitigating factor.

Nina grabbed her phone and googled JL Knight. A torrent of results crowded the small screen. She started with the facts:

> *Julian Leroy Knight is an English actor. He is best known for his starring role in* Thunder, *directed by George Kirby.*

Then she searched for the fluff. There was so much of it: fan art, photographs, video, essays and articles. Nina swiped through photos of the actor posing on the red carpet to snapshots of the man stretched out all but naked on a beach. However, the most recent photo was of him, hunched low, handing a handsome black cat to an ecstatic little girl. It had a clever little caption: *JL Knight literally saves the cat!* There were batches of cheerful on-camera interviews and one grainy thirty-second clip of a young JL Knight, drunk at a Hollywood party, with a message for the critics who'd panned his debut feature film: "Kiss my ass!"

Celebrity gossip sites provided relationship status updates (*Love Is Dead: JL Knight and Bettina Ford Have Split*) and chronicled professional setbacks (*JL Knight— of "Kiss My Ass" Infamy—Gets His Ass Kicked at Box Office*). A few more clicks and Nina landed on a blog dedicated to the film industry that put it all in context. JL Knight's ex-girlfriend and former costar, Bettina Ford, had spearheaded a boycott of his latest release after most of her scenes were cut in postproduction. The movie had flopped.

And, to top it all off, she came across a devastating profile of the actor in *Vanities*, titled *Nite Nite, JL Knight*.

*The star's brand of toxic masculinity should have
gone the way of the Hummer. His bloated films
glorify violence, celebrate hypermasculine culture
and belittle women. The actor is famous for his portrayal of an assassin for hire (code name "Thunder") in the film adaptation of a once-popular video
game. In the films, he stops at nothing to fulfill a
contract, sometimes destroying entire cities to wipe
out one target. Having not made much of his talent,
content to feed from the bottom of the Hollywood
swamp, JL Knight ought to retire.*

Well, damn.

Nina, a reader, writer and theater geek, was not one
to line up for a big Hollywood release. A regular at her
neighborhood's art house movie theater, she preferred
her movies with subtitles. All this fuss about an action
movie seemed a bit much. A fast-paced, high-voltage
action flick served a purpose and had a place on the
entertainment spectrum—particularly at the end of a
long, hard day. On the other hand, why cut the scenes
of a female character? Who'd made that call? Representation mattered, and she would've supported a boycott.

A new-message alert popped up on her phone screen.
It was a much-awaited email from her literary agent.

Had lunch with editor today. She passed on the short
story collection BUT expressed great interest in a follow-up to Backstage Diva. This is promising. Let's have
lunch next week and discuss.

Nina moaned. Another memoir? She was done with
all that. *Backstage Diva* chronicled her experience

growing up in Manhattan, the daughter of a Broadway actress. The book tour had been torture. She'd had to crisscross America answering intrusive questions from strangers that she would have never entertained otherwise. That was the price she had to pay for offering up details of her family life for public consumption. She'd vowed never to do it again.

"Ugh!" she cried up to the ceiling. The vaulted ceiling was fresco-free, not one rosy-cheeked angel to be found—a disappointment.

Nina kicked off her shoes, stacked a couple throw pillows under her head and sank into the couch. *Thunder* was available for streaming, and because this qualified as a long, hard day, she slipped on her headphones and hit Play.

The best room at Sand Castle didn't guarantee rest. Julian was stretched out on his back on the comically large bed, staring at the painted ceiling and wondered who, in their right mind, would want to have sex with angels staring down at them.

He closed his eyes, desperate for sleep. Two days ago, he'd woken up in California to the threat of wildfire overtaking his neighborhood. The view from his bedroom window was walled off with smoke. On a clear day he could see as far as the Pacific.

He'd turned on the television and checked his phone for information. The news headlines were short, capturing the general state of panic. *Brush Fire Erupts. Brush Fire Doubles in Size. Fire Changes Course.* An evacuation order was in effect for the Hollywood Hills. His landlord sent him a text message in all caps to reinforce it. GET PACKING! Since his landlord was also his neighbor, he couldn't ignore the directive.

It had irked him to abandon his house, only it wasn't his to stay and defend. The modern home, nestled in the Hollywood Hills, was a rental. He'd moved in after his breakup. The house had come fully furnished. Most of his personal belongings were still in storage, which made packing a breeze. Julian folded his clothes into two large suitcases and tossed in his toiletries. He gathered his laptop, tablet, camera, personal phone and burner phone. He emptied the contents of his file cabinet into a messenger bag. The only thing left to do was return the cat.

Wasabi, his neighbor's green-eyed cat, would be asleep under his car. As per their routines, Julian popped open the trunk of his black Ferrari and the cat sprang out. He scooped him up. It would only take a minute to deliver him to Rosie, the neighbor's nanny.

The night he'd moved into the neighborhood, Julian had caught Rosie lighting a cigarette in the gazebo. At his approach she'd leaped to her feet, knocking a planter on its side. She hid the hand with the cigarette behind her back, but a curl of smoke rose above her head.

"Are you supposed to be here?" he asked.

Her eyes widened. "Holy mother! You're JL Knight!"

"I know who I am."

"I'm not trespassing, sir," she said. "I'm the nanny from next door. I come over once a week to do some light housekeeping."

She was older than him by a decade—and a Brit. Julian asked her to drop the "sir."

"Please don't tell my employer you caught me smoking. He doesn't hire smokers."

Her employer was his landlord. Julian told her to

relax. The day he caused a hardworking woman to lose a job was the day his mother would turn in her grave—she who only wanted to rest in peace in her homeland of Jamaica. He and Rosie had been friends ever since. He would not have wanted to evacuate without first checking on her, and Wasabi gave him the perfect excuse.

Julian accessed the neighboring property by a side gate. If not for the threat of flames and the low-hanging clouds of smoke, it was a peaceful morning. He made his way to the front door, passing a U-Haul truck parked in the U-shaped driveway. Rosie threw open the door before he had a chance to ring the doorbell. "JL Knight, you're my hero!" she exclaimed. "You've saved me the trouble of mounting a search party for that cat."

"Next time check my garage," he said. "That's where he'll be. Do you still have the code?"

While Rosie checked to make sure her information was up to date, a little blonde girl came barreling into the foyer, squealing with joy at the sight of Wasabi. Julian knelt until they were almost eye level and put the cat in her arms.

Rosie plucked her phone from her uniform pocket and snapped a photo. "How precious! Samantha, say thank you to Mr. Knight."

The little girl offered a shy smile. "Tanks."

Julian ruffled her hair and unfolded to his full height. Then he asked Rosie if she planned to evacuate with her employers.

"We're heading to the house in Palm Springs," she said. "It's a fixer, so we'll be roughing it. How about you?"

"I'm ready to roll out." Julian had no definite plans. There were calls for donations to the fire department—

water bottles and eye drops, mostly. He'd see to that and then possibly check into a hotel until it was safe to return. He had no place to be, really.

Rosie asked Samantha to find Wasabi's favorite toy and accompanied him down the front steps.

"I've been meaning to talk to you, JL Knight," she said. "Now seems like the right time."

Julian winced at her use of his stage name. He'd asked her one hundred times to stop calling him that, but with Rosie it was either "sir" or "JL Knight." This confirmed what he'd known to be true for some time. For some people, no matter what he did, he'd be indistinguishable from his acting persona. For years, he hadn't minded. He was best known for his role in *Thunder*. The character had served him well and made him rich, but now he couldn't shake him. Not that there would be any more *Thunder* movies. The third had bombed so badly at the box office there was no talk of a fourth installment. One day they'd reboot the franchise with another, younger actor and he'd be forgotten.

Rosie linked her arm through his, and they walked down the path to the side gate. "I'm in no position to give you life advice."

"I wouldn't be so sure," Julian replied.

Rosie was a practical-minded woman. In England, she'd run a playgroup in her home, but she'd found that looking after of the kids of the Hollywood elite was more financially rewarding. "They think I'm Mary bloody Poppins," she'd confided one night. She planned to retire in five years once she had enough saved away to buy a cottage in her hometown. Her life was in order. By comparison, his life was a mess.

"All this free time is not good for you. Get back to work."

"It's not that simple." Julian's agent wasn't returning his calls.

"It is, actually. You're too smart and talented to waste your time."

They'd reached the end of the path, and Julian felt a wave of relief. He recognized the truth when he heard it, and the truth wasn't something he was equipped to deal with right now. He was running from an actual fire—no time to run from existential ones, too.

He faced Rosie and rested his chin on the top of her head. "Tanks."

She pushed him away and called him a softie. Julian marched home and blamed his stinging eyes on the smoke that thickened the air. He loaded his bags in the trunk of his car and went back inside the house for one last thing. From a bottom dresser drawer, he pulled out a dog-eared copy of a screenplay well into its ninth revision. *Midnight Sun*. He flipped it open, thumbed through it, shook his head, then tucked it under his arm.

While he locked up the house, Julian got his assistant, Katia, on the phone. "Hey, Kat. Heading to Miami in the morning. Could you charter a plane and book a suite at Sand Castle?"

"Only if I can bum a ride. I'm heading to Boca for the holiday."

Oh, right. Independence Day. "I'll be there for a bit longer, but I'd welcome the company on the flight out."

"How much longer?" she asked.

She needed this information to book the hotel, only he couldn't give her exact dates. "A month or so."

"You're not retiring to Florida, are you?"

"No. The opposite."

She let out a grumpy sound. "Okay. Fine."

His next call was to an independent film producer who had once expressed interest in his project. When Julian had finally backed out of his garage, he didn't get far. A police checkpoint at the foot of the Hills slowed the flow of traffic, but he felt as if he were going places.

Julian grabbed his phone and played a few rounds of the sort of game that would have solidified his reputation as a warmonger. He lost the final round, slipped off his headphones and listened for sounds of the woman locked away in the adjoining room. Ms. Taylor. She claimed to be a writer. Time to find out. He typed "female author Taylor" in a search engine and filtered the results by image. He swiped through dozens of photos of Taylors, including Taylor Swift, but there was only one professional headshot of a dark-skinned, brown-eyed beauty.

In the photograph, she looked straight at the camera with a measured smile. She wore red lipstick and her black hair fell straight and loose, framing her face. The caption read: *Nina Taylor, memoirist, NYT Review of Books.*

*I'm only really qualified to write about myself.* He recalled her words. They hadn't made sense at the time. They did now. Julian reached for a second pillow and wedged it under his head. He was about to jump down the internet rabbit hole and might as well get comfortable.

One hour later, he'd read several reviews of her memoir, *Backstage Diva*, and listened to snippets of podcast interviews. He'd watched a panel discussion on memoir writing on Book TV. She was one of three panelists, but by far the most remarkable. He'd learned the following:

A) Nina Taylor was the daughter of a deceased stage actress celebrated for her Tony-nominated portrayal of Beneatha Younger in a 1999 Broadway revival of *A Raisin in the Sun*.

B) Nina was a respected artist in her own right with a bestselling memoir and several published magazine articles.

C) Nina was single, lived in New York City and was working on a collection of short stories.

There was only one thing left to do. He purchased *Backstage Diva*, the audiobook, with one click. Then he adjusted his headphones and hit Play.

# Four

Nina had dozed off on the couch halfway through the movie. She woke up to the sound of screeching tires, a car chase in full swing. She sat up and massaged a kink in her neck. If the Garden Room was still unavailable, they had better find her something! She had no intention of spending the night on a sleeper sofa while JL Knight slept in luxury. If Sand Castle couldn't accommodate her, she was leaving. She'd arrange a ride to the airport, hop on any flight and get the heck out of the Sunshine State. *Sorry, Mom. I'll light a candle or burn sage and celebrate your life...at home.*

Her room opened to the hallway. Nina slipped out and took the stairs to the courtyard. The front desk clerk had no answers, so she marched to Grace Guzman's office. When her knock went unanswered, Nina was certain nothing would be resolved tonight. Angry and aimless,

she wandered along the cloisters, coming across an enclosed garden. It was small but lush. Mesmerized by
the fairy lights creating the illusion of a starry sky, she
traveled down a gravel path and somehow missed the
bronze statue at the center of the garden. She struck her
foot against the granite pedestal, fell to the ground and
yelped like a dog.

She choked on a sob. Had she flown to Miami just to
make a fool of herself?

Rhythmic applause, sharp and slow, rose up from
deep in the garden. Nina scrambled to her feet and wiped
away the blades of grass stuck to her cheek. When she
was presentable, she scrutinized the shadows and saw,
quite clearly, Grace Guzman staring back at her. Grace
sat in a rattan chair, hair loosened from the bun she'd
sported earlier. Besides her was a low table with a pitcher
of red sangria and a couple of wineglasses. Say what you
want, the woman had style.

"You're quite the performance artist, Ms. Taylor."

Off-duty Grace was even bitchier than on-duty Grace.
How was that possible?

Nina pointed to the statue. "This thing is a hazard."

"The goddess is not a hazard."

"Goddess?"

"Aphrodite," Grace said, as if it were obvious.

Nina examined Aphrodite. Hunched low to the
ground, her demure pose struck Nina as unnatural—
Aphrodite being the goddess of love and beauty and all.
Shouldn't she stand tall?

"Have a seat, Ms. Taylor," Grace said. "That statue
will be here long after you've gone."

Those words put everything in perspective. This man-

sion had seen war, economic depression and ecologic ca-
tastrophe. Aphrodite was no stranger to drama.

Her chin held high, Nina hobbled over to the offered
seat. Grace poured a glass of sangria and handed it over
as if it were the cure for all things. Then she folded her
hands on her lap and waited for Nina to explain herself.
If there was a goddess in this garden, it wasn't Aphrodite.

When Nina wasn't forthcoming, Grace broke the silence. "I like to sit here in the early evenings. The guests
are getting ready for dinner and the hotel tends to be
quiet."

The hotel was as quiet as could be expected with the
street noise drilling through the wall of high shrubs.
Nina raked her brain for something to say. "This is a
beautiful garden. The lights are a nice touch."

"We were supposed to host a wedding here tonight.
It was canceled."

"That's awful."

"The couple was eloping," Grace said with a sigh.
"Never a good sign."

Nina disagreed. "Not every bride needs an entourage."

"Yes, but for some it takes a village," Grace said.
"They need a nagging mother, a dozen bridesmaids and
a minimum of fifty guests to get them to the altar. I
know I did."

"My mother is dead."

The words spilled out without warning. Fragments of
her mother's obit surfaced in her memory. Estelle Taylor,
star of *A Raisin in the Sun* and *Porgy and Bess*, died of
pneumonia in New York City on July 3. She was sixty.

"I'm sorry to hear it, Ms. Taylor."

"Oh, never mind." Nina dabbed at the corner of her eyes. "It's been a year. I don't know why I brought it up."

"Does it matter if it's been a year or ten?" Grace asked.

"No."

"Please don't take this the wrong way," Grace said, "but you look exhausted. Get some rest tonight."

"I don't have a room!" she reminded Grace. "I'm on a sofa bed in the study! How restful will that be?"

"You and Mr. Knight came up with this solution on your own."

"I didn't think it through," Nina said.

"Had you let me do my job, I would have offered you accommodations at any one of our hotel partners."

Had Grace done her job, she wouldn't have given away Nina's suite to JL Knight. But she was too exhausted to belabor the point. "Is that still an option?"

It was a holiday weekend, and she assumed most hotels were booked solid.

"It is. But you should know the sofa bed is very comfortable. It's imported from Italy." Grace stood to leave. "I'll leave instructions with the front desk. Whatever you do, don't delay."

"Because of the holiday?"

"Because of the rain."

As soon as Grace spoke the words, a gust a wind swirled through the garden trailing the scent of rain. A clap of thunder had Nina jumping to her feet.

Nina was out of breath when she made it back to the third floor, just narrowly escaping a downpour. She entered the suite through the sitting room. The doors to the balcony were wide-open and there he was, standing with his back to her. Without the added layer of a jacket, she could plainly see the contours of his muscles under his T-shirt, and it was impressive—not that she cared.

Nina drew a breath for courage and joined him on the balcony, leaning against the rail. He smiled down at her, and she noticed that his soft brown eyes were flecked with gold. How had she not noticed before?

"There you are, Goldilocks."

Nina cringed, but only on the inside. On the outside, she remained cool. "I spoke to the manager. They can put me up at another hotel."

"You'd head out in the rain?"

"I love rain." It was Miami! Summer showers were part of the package.

"What do you love? Singing in it? Dancing in it?"

"None of the above." The sound of it was enough.

"Hate to *rain* on your exit parade, but if anyone is leaving, it's me."

"I just think—"

"Stop thinking," he said, interrupting, and yet his voice was gentle. "We agreed to make the best of this. Don't flake on me now."

Her gaze fell to his hands gripping the rail. In the movie, he'd gripped the steering wheel of his sports car in the same way. To take her mind off the soft color of his eyes, his gentle voice, firm grip and sculpted arms, Nina turned away and focused on the view. The palm trees swayed in the rain. Below, a cluster of tourists stood outside the hotel gates. Once dubbed the *Playboy* Mansion of the South, it was a Miami Beach tradition to pose on the stone steps—even in the pouring rain.

"Did I ever tell you about the time I worked here as a valet attendant?"

She had read about that online, but she couldn't tell him that. "When would you have told me, JL Knight? We've just met."

"Call me Julian," he said. "Trash this hotel suite if you like. I don't care. But I insist you call me Julian."

"In that case, *Julian*, I insist you call me Nina," she said. "Call me Goldilocks one more time and I'll throw you off this balcony."

"I'd like to see you try." He stretched lazily. "Nina is a pretty name."

The unexpected compliment threw her off guard. She felt herself softening and couldn't allow that. "We're off topic, *Julian*. I'll stay the night, but I'll probably leave in the morning."

"Tomorrow's the Fourth," he said. "Won't that ruin your holiday?"

Her holiday was ruined. There was no use pretending that it wasn't. "I'll buy a hot dog at the airport. That should do it."

"You'll be missing the pool party," he said. "Grace says it's not to be missed."

This day had been so draining, so bizarre, that she hadn't even made it to the hotel pool. How sad was that?

Julian's phone rang in his pocket. He reached for it and answered right away.

"I know, I know," he said, laughing at whatever the caller had said. "Soon! Promise! But tomorrow won't work. How about the day after that? Would you be up for it?"

Nina turned away, pretending as if she weren't listening. The winds picked up and tossed her braid about like threadbare rope. Julian wrapped a hand around her elbow and steered her inside, still carrying on his conversation. "You don't have to sell me on it. I want to come, and I miss your cooking." He shut the door behind them. "All the flowers you want. Promise."

Nina crossed the sitting room to her door. Julian's conversation was taking an intimate turn, and it made her uncomfortable. But when he spoke up again, she knew he was addressing her.

"Have you eaten?"

She turned in time to see him pocketing his phone. "I'm not hungry."

She had a couple protein bars and airline pretzels stashed in her purse. She'd make a meal out of it. More than anything, she wanted to lock herself in her room, fold out the bed and sleep for twelve hours straight. She wanted to say good-night and disappear behind a shut door, but a nagging feeling kept her rooted in place. She had something to get off her chest.

"Julian, I'm not a crazy person in real life."

"Okay," he said. "You just play one on TV?"

"Something like that."

Nina might never be able to correct his first impression of her. Back in Hollywood, he'd likely entertain his friends with the story. "Did I tell you about the time I walked into a hotel room in Miami to find a woman taking a selfie on my bed?" And they'd all laugh.

He sat on the arm of a wing chair and leveled those golden-brown eyes on her. "Why did you do it?"

"You mean sneak into your room, climb on your bed and pose for a selfie?"

He nodded. "That sums it up."

"Who wouldn't? It's a gorgeous room, don't you think?"

"No. Not really," he said. "Too many gold knick-knacks for my taste."

She agreed. There were way too many knickknacks, period. She wished she could leave it at that, but the truth was clawing at her throat. It would choke her if she didn't speak up. Nina had to share the burden with someone. Julian was right there, watching her, waiting for more. She might as well tell him. "It was my mother's dream to stay at this hotel. She'd go on and on about the Oasis. Her idols had all spent the night here—Elizabeth, Marilyn, Diana, Aretha… My mom had extravagant dreams."

Nina had planned this trip to mark the one-year anniversary of her mother's passing. She had wanted to do something to honor the late actress's life, something other than showing up at her grave with flowers.

Julian's gaze softened. "Want to switch rooms?"

"No," Nina said firmly. She'd gone too far with this already. "And don't argue with me. I'm too tired."

"Want to come in and take that selfie?"

Nina smiled despite herself. "No, thanks."

She opened the door to her room. The brass doorknob jammed, so the movement wasn't as smooth as she would have liked. "Good night, Julian."

He was still watching her with that same unwavering interest, as if she fascinated and confused him all at once. "Good night, Nina."

She shut the door and collapsed against it. She was hungry and a little light-headed. That was all. However, the feeling stayed, even after she'd eaten, showered, detangled and braided her hair.

Nina pulled out the bed and sat up cross-legged. A minute later, she got up and poured herself a glass of water. Outside, it was raining still, and the wet windowpanes glistened in the moonlight. She picked up her phone from the charger and took it to bed with her. Earlier, she'd skipped past the more revealing photos of her roommate online. Now she believed they were worth a second look. She found a trove of glossy photos taken on location in Italy's Amalfi Coast for a *British Vogue* editorial. Some of the photos were candid shots taken during breaks. Nina tapped on one to enlarge it. Wearing dark sunglasses and a towel flung around his neck, skin baked to a golden brown, Julian stood palling around with the crewmen. In another, he was stretched out on the hard, flat sand, one arm across his eyes shielding them from the sun. He looked thoroughly relaxed, not pressed for time, not pressed for anything. His long limbs looked heavy.

Nina hoped his skin tasted like salt.

# Five

Julian's car pulled up the drive to the Coconut Grove estate. Nestled among mature oaks was the modern home of Francisco Cortes. Julian asked his hotel-appointed driver to come back around in a couple of hours, then climbed the steps leading to the porch. A housekeeper greeted Julian at the door and led him to a back patio. The silver-haired man with the profile that ought to be minted on coins steered forward in a motorized chair. His lips split into a smile. "This is an honor. Welcome to Miami."

Over lunch, they discussed the California wildfires, at last under control. "With the sea levels rising," Julian said, "you must worry—"

Francisco interrupted him midsentence. "You and I are not going to solve climate change, not today. So why don't you tell me why you're here?"

Julian took a gulp of water. This would be the first time he discussed his project with anyone, and he was nervous. "I'm here to shoot my first film."

"Going independent," Francisco said. "JL Knight Productions… That's got a nice ring to it."

Julian didn't dispute it, but he'd settled on Knight Films.

"Good luck to you," Francisco said. "I mean it. In my day, when the business spit you out, you were done. So I admire what you're doing. But here's the thing— if you've come to offer me the role of the grandpa with the heart of gold, you can forget it. I've retired. I don't play grandpas. I sure as hell don't play characters with hearts of gold."

Julian sat back in his chair and considered the clear-eyed man opposite him. He'd come to the right place. "I've come to ask you to direct."

"You might have inhaled a little too much smoke in the fire," Francisco said, deadpan.

"Back in '91, you made a short film that debuted in Toronto."

Francisco dismissed his words with a wave of a hand. "That was just for fun."

"Fun is what I'm after," Julian said. "I watched it five times. As I've watched all your films."

"Not all of them, I hope," Francisco said with a chuckle. "Some of them were trash."

Francisco Cortes had played the quintessential Latin lover in countless films. He was magnetic on camera, commanding every scene he was in. But a near-fatal car accident had left him disabled and killed his career.

"Wouldn't you have liked to direct given the chance?" Julian asked.

"Well, now." Francisco ran his fingers along his well-trimmed goatee. "If anyone had predicted that I'd be having this discussion with JL Knight, I wouldn't have believed them."

"That's 'cause you're not." Julian felt compelled to reintroduce himself at every turn, like some parody of James Bond. "I'm Julian. You can forget JL."

"Don't wipe out your legacy. On winter nights we screen movies out here." He made a gesture capturing the world within the coral rock wall surrounding the estate: his home, the garden with its tangles of tropical plants, a kidney-shaped pool and a hot tub fitted under a pergola. "*Thunder* is always a crowd pleaser."

Julian clasped his hands together. "Happy to hear it."

"Tell me about your project."

Years ago, a UCLA film school student and waiter at one of his favorite taco spots had pitched Julian a story based on a true crime set in LA. The half-baked pitch was a nonstarter, but it had planted a seed in Julian's mind. On and off, he'd worked on a script of his own set in Miami. *Midnight Sun* was a heist film loosely based on the story of a Miami heiress who fell victim to her con-artist boyfriend.

"Yeah… I read about that," Francisco said. "He stole her jewels during a solar eclipse."

"Hence the title."

"And you'd play the con artist."

"That's the idea," Julian said. "It's a supporting role. This heiress is the lead."

"Very smart. You plan to film here in Miami?"

Julian relaxed into his chair. Francisco was asking all the right questions. "Can't do it convincingly anywhere else."

"Florida doesn't offer tax incentives," Francisco said. "Broward County has a program. You might want to consider filming some scenes there."

Julian was open to anything, so long as he could shoot some scenes at Sand Castle.

"I'll make a few calls. Find out what kinds of incentives are out there," Francisco said. "Meanwhile, send me the script."

"Thought you'd never ask." Julian pulled a copy of the screenplay from his leather messenger bag and handed it over. "If you'd like an electronic copy, just give me your email address."

Francisco flipped through the pages. "You wrote this?"

Julian mumbled his answer, fearful of Francisco's reaction. What if he thought it a joke and withdrew his support? But the older man chuckled good-naturedly. "You surprise me, Julian."

For the next couple of hours, they discussed financing and distribution options. Julian had reached out to a production company and had secured some financing. Francisco had not committed to the project, but he promised to help raise more funds and support Julian in every possible way.

"What are your plans for today?" Francisco asked. "I'm having a family cookout. You're welcome to join us."

"Thanks, but I'm meeting with friends."

With that lie, Julian ended the meeting. He was not in the holiday cookout or party mood. His driver, a young guy who went only by Pete, was waiting outside. Kat had secured his services for the duration of his stay. On the drive back to the hotel, he asked question after question until Julian slipped on his earphones to signal the Q&A session was over. The rest of the ride was blissfully quiet and, by the time he got back to Sand Castle, he'd received good news and bad news via text message.

The good news was from Francisco. He'd immediately reached out to friends at a local arts foundation and put in an informal request for grant funding. "They won't turn me down." The bad news was from Kat. A photo of him and Nina Taylor had surfaced on social media. It was a grainy cell phone pic of the two of them on the balcony.

In the photo, they were staring at each other. Julian was dropped back in time to the moment Nina had threatened to toss him over the balcony if he called her Goldilocks again. She was looking up at him with a glint of defiance in her eyes. He'd loved the display of bravado and it showed on his face. The social media caption read: *Kiss Already!*

Julian let out a sigh. He only had himself to blame. He knew better than to stand on an open balcony within cell phone camera range in the company of a woman. The cover of darkness plus a veil of rainfall was no cover at all. He'd have to warn Nina. He did not want her to be blindsided.

This gave him the perfect excuse to knock on her door. Every cloud, a silver lining…

He knocked, but there was no answer. The famous pool party was raging downstairs, and he decided to check it out. Not because he thought it would be fun to celebrate the Fourth with a bunch of drunken strangers, and not because he enjoyed being passed around like a photo booth prop, which was sure to happen, but in the vague hopes that she might be there.

Downstairs, he was ushered without question beyond the velvet ropes. He ignored the assortment of vodka on display at the bar and ordered a gin and tonic. Out of the corner of his eye, he spotted a woman elbowing her way toward him, and he readied himself. Holding up her camera, she begged for a photo. "My boyfriend will die. He's your number one fan." Women seldom admitted to liking his films. It was always a husband, boyfriend or brother who got them to the theater.

The bartender volunteered to take the photo. He was a fan as well. With so many fans, Julian wondered how his film had flopped. Then he grabbed his drink and moved away from the bar. From his vantage point on the veranda, he scanned the crowd below. It was possible that Nina had done the reasonable thing—checked out of the hotel and flown home. But then he spotted her on the dance floor, and it was clear to him that reason wasn't the fuel she was running on.

Julian didn't make a move—he couldn't. In the short time he'd known her, he'd seen her angry, distraught, threatening and resigned. But here was a side of her that he hadn't guessed existed, and he was riveted. Nina was playful, dancing freely and having fun. But then he noticed the tight set of her jaw. Her movements were forced. He recalled what she'd told him the night before. He'd lost his mother years ago and knew exactly what she was going through. He'd been in Hawaii filming a special crossover episode of *Riverside Rescue* when he'd learned of his mother's untimely death. The loss had sent him reeling for months.

Julian lost sight of Nina. When he spotted her again,

she was standing dangerously close to the edge of the pool, throwing back a shot of the night's signature vodka. She wore a little white dress held up by thin straps. Her hair fell in loose waves past her shoulders. Her dark skin gleamed in the soft light of the setting sun. She was so bloody beautiful.

He raced down the stairs and forged a path toward her despite mounting doubts. *Leave her alone. She doesn't need you.* Then a few things happened to erase his concerns. A rocket exploded overhead, causing the crowd to compress and swell. Nina lost her balance and tipped backward into the still waters of the pool and vanished. It was possible that he was the only one who'd seen it, and now there was no question that she needed him.

*He's not my type.*

Nina had spotted Julian the moment he'd entered the upper-level VIP veranda, the same she'd been turned away from an hour earlier. She'd had to access the party at the general population entrance by the lower-level pool. Although the whole ordeal had irritated her to no end, her irritations were washed away when a hostess presented her with an array of fruit-flavored vodka shots to choose from.

She'd slept well the night before—either the sofa bed was surprisingly comfortable or she'd been too exhausted to notice the difference. In any case, she woke up with a clear head and realized that attempting to travel on the Fourth of July was plain dumb. She had the suite to herself. Julian had set out early—she'd heard him fumbling around in the sitting area actively trying not to make noise. Once he left, Nina ordered room service and sat at the antique desk to write in her journal.

But she'd refused to stay cooped up in her room while a party was in full swing outside.

Nina was relieved that Julian had not yet returned when she left the suite in her made-for-a-Miami-(or Vegas)-pool-party minidress. And yet she was doubly relieved when she spotted him on the VIP veranda. She'd enjoyed the quiet in the suite, but there was such a thing as too much quiet. She had missed his voice. And then she watched as he pulled a bikini-clad beauty into a hug. Her mouth went dry, and she turned away in search of more fruit-flavored vodka.

*Whatever. He's not my type.*

She went for clean-cut lawyer/stockbroker types. Men who couldn't bench-press anything heavier than a laptop but still managed to wear suits beautifully. Julian Knight in his jeans and tees worn mostly to show off his sculpted body was the opposite of that.

Assessing the attractiveness of one action hero on the scale of lawyer to stockbroker was an insane waste of time. She was at a party crowded with men! Nina infiltrated a squad of women on the dance floor. The DJ played the summer hits, and above them the sky was turning purple. She laughed at the crazy moves of her new friends and matched them with moves of her own. Soon, though, the crowd swallowed her up. She searched around for the others, but the group had dismantled.

The dance floor stretched alongside the pool, and Nina danced her way toward it. She took a breath. *I'm tipsy*, she admitted, and scooped another glass from a passing waiter's tray. *Might as well get good and drunk.* She sent coconut-flavored vodka down her throat in one gulp then clutched the empty shot glass to her chest.

Still, the words crawled across the ticker of her mind. *He's just not my type.*

The first rocket of the night surged into the sky and exploded; the sound ripped through the night. While everyone welcomed the burst of sound and color with cheers, Nina startled, lost her balance and toppled cleanly into the deep end of pool. It was a relief, frankly. The news ticker in her brain went dark.

# Six

Nina stood shivering in the chilly marble bathroom. From the other side of the door, Julian asked whether she was decent. She tightened the towel around her torso and the one wrapped around her head before answering yes. He handed her a hotel robe and slippers through a crack in the doorway. All she could think was: *This man has seen me naked.*

This man had also dived into a pool to fish her out, carried her through the party crowd guided by the flash of hundreds of camera phones and whisked her up to their suite via private elevator. All the while, she'd coughed up water on his chest. Once in their room, he'd helped her out of her dress. The zipper gave way easily enough, but the soaked fabric had clung to her like suction wrap. Then he'd assisted her into the shower.

Nina attempted to blow-dry her hair. The noise aggravated her pounding headache and she gave up, letting her hair fall damp down her back. And since she could not think of anything more to do to stall the inevitable, she slipped on the robe and stepped out to face him.

He was waiting just outside the door, his face soft with concern. "Hey. Come lie down."

"Here?" Nina flatly refused. "That's fine. I'll head to my room now."

She bolted toward the bedroom door, but her tortoise's pace made it easy for him to block her. All he had to do was step in her path. "I'm going to order tea and soup and whatever else you like. It'll make things easier if you camp out here."

That sounded reasonable enough. Not the part about the soup, though. That sounded terrible. Nevertheless, it felt wrong to give in to him. "My things are in my room and…" She winced with pain. Her headache intensified with each word of false protest. Between the drinking and the drowning, she had no energy left to argue.

He linked an arm around her waist and assisted her onto the large, inviting bed. Tonight, it was covered in a hunter-green bedspread embroidered in gold.

"What things do you need?" he asked. "I'll grab them for you."

She wanted to ask for her journal. Instead, she asked for her bag of toiletries on the bathroom vanity. Julian left and returned in a flash with her toiletries, her phone that she'd left charging in her room, her monogrammed slippers from J. Crew *and* her journal. She thanked him enthusiastically, and yet he didn't look pleased.

"What's the matter?" she asked.

"Don't tell me you slept on a couch last night." His voice was flat.

"The couch converts into a bed." When his eyes widened in disbelief, she added, "Don't worry. It's imported from Italy and very comfortable."

He placed her slippers at the side of the bed. "You said this suite had two bedrooms. That's not a bedroom. That's a study."

"Shows you how much I know."

He stood over her, a frown tugging at his lips. Nina wasn't comfortable with him handling her journal, so she pried it out of his hands. "I'll take this. Thanks."

"You're spending the night here," he said. "It's my turn on the couch."

"Don't be ridiculous." Nina checked her phone to better give the impression that she was fine and everything was good. There were a few social media alerts, but she ignored them.

"If it's so comfortable, what's the problem?"

"I'm not putting you out of your bedroom. And that's that."

"Why not?" He poured her a glass of water then riffled through a leather case on the dresser for a bottle of Tylenol. "You have a stronger claim to it than I do."

"Yeah, but you're paying for it," she said. "You *are* paying for it, right, JL Knight?"

He handed her the glass and two pills. She lifted her head off the pillow, but that was all she could manage.

"Need an extra pillow, Goldie?" he said with a smirk. But seeing that she was truly struggling, he stepped forward and scooped the back of her head in his palm. "Lean on me," he said. "Now open wide." He dropped the pills in her mouth, and Nina wondered why her imagination was running wild with those two simple commands. He held the glass to her lips. "Swallow."

When he lowered her onto the pillows, there was no question where she was spending the night.

He ordered food: mint tea for her, a veggie burger for him and extra fries for them to share. He hung up and looked at her intently. "You okay?"

"I'm fine," she said. "This is a lot of fuss. I fell into a pool. That's all."

Her words did not seem to reach him. "Don't get out of bed. I'll open for room service when they get here."

"Don't tell me what to do."

"Don't be difficult." He left to take a shower, waving goodbye.

As soon as the bathroom door shut behind him, Nina reached for her journal out of habit. A hotel logo pen was tucked in the pages. She chewed on the cap for a minute, then jotted the first thing that came to mind.

*Welcome to Rock Bottom! Hope you stay awhile.*

It killed her that she'd had to be rescued by JL Knight like some damsel in distress. How did she get to this place? She had not been herself these last few days. It was as if she were on an emotional roller coaster: throwing tantrums, sneaking into hotel rooms, crashing into statues and now this!

She listened to the sounds of the shower. When Julian came out of the bathroom in a clean T-shirt and soft sweatpants, he looked fresh. She likely looked as bad as she felt, because he rushed over.

"Oh, come on, love. Don't do that." He sat next to her and stroked a lock of hair away from her wet cheek. "Don't cry."

Nina jerked away. His touch hadn't startled her, but his words had. Was she crying? Julian recoiled from her in one smooth ripple of muscle. She caught him by the hand before he got away. "It's okay. You startled me, that's all."

He nodded but stayed quiet. She gave his hand a little squeeze. "Thanks for rescuing me and...stuff."

God knew she owed him a debt of gratitude for all the "stuff" she was too embarrassed to mention now.

He shrugged. "Anyone would have done it."

"No one else did. Just you," Nina said. "So, thanks."

"You're welcome." His face remained impassive, but she caught a glint in his eyes. The room went warm. Nina fought the impulse to shed the plush robe as images of him half-naked on the coast of Italy flooded her mind. She blinked the images away as he went to sit at the far end of the bed, as far from her as he could manage without falling to the ground.

"Listen, Julian, I have something to say, and it's important."

"I'm listening."

"I don't want to have sex with you."

"You're in good company," he said. "The queue of women who don't want to have sex with me goes around the block."

"Okay, then. I'll get in line."

"And take a number," he added. "I like to keep things orderly."

JL Knight was self-deprecating and funny. Why hadn't any of this gotten into the *Vanities* article?

"All this is to say, we can share this bed," Nina said. "It's as large as a continent. There's room enough for the both of us."

"We could build a wall, line pillows from top to bottom?" he suggested.

She nodded in agreement. "I've heard walls are super effective."

And they laughed like kids until room service arrived with the food. Julian prepared her tea and set up a tray with her fries—the only effective cure for drunkenness. Nina's headache was dissipating. How could she feel bad when she was receiving such excellent care? Her eyes drifted up to the angels floating above. She'd drowned, died and gone to heaven. That was the only explanation that made sense.

Julian dragged a wingback chair over to the bed and settled in to eat his burger. Between greedy bites, he explained that he'd been raised vegetarian. He only ate meat on occasion.

"What's your deal?" she asked. "Are you here to film a movie?"

"That's classified information, Nina Taylor."

"You don't trust me," she said. "Even now. After everything we've been through. I trust you with my life."

"That's because you've seen me in action," he said. "You know what I can do."

He had a point. "Here's the thing—I don't have the energy to keep up this tit for tat. I trust you...enough. Could we just be friends now?"

"My friendship is a complicated thing." He picked up his phone, scrolled for a bit and handed it to her. "I'll show you what I mean."

Someone by the handle @TheAimlessDayTripper had posted a photo of her and Julian standing on the balcony, facing each other, gazing into each other's eyes. Caption: *Kiss Already!* The post had 5,470 likes.

She returned his phone. "That's not so bad."

He tapped the screen and showed her a video of him

lifting her out of the pool, water pouring off his back. Her face was buried in his chest, and for that she was grateful. Caption: *#RescueMeJLK*

Nina passed him the phone with a nervous laugh. She couldn't look at the photos or video without cringing. There was something about them, something indefinable. Everyone was picking up on it.

Julian fell back into the chair and read her a tweet. "'JLK sliced through the crowd, dived into the pool and emerged the hero cradling the drowning woman in his arms. #RescueMeJLK.'"

Nina repeated the hashtag. "Like from that time you saved the cat!"

He looked up at her from the screen, brows drawn in confusion. "What cat?"

Nina stuffed her mouth with fries. She couldn't answer that question without admitting that she'd googled him.

"I didn't rescue any cat," he said. "Does that even sound like me?"

"How would I know?" She reminded him, again, that they'd just met.

"You keep reaching for that tired excuse."

"Anyway. There's a picture of you returning some little girl's cat."

"Wasabi? That old goat didn't need saving."

He sounded genuinely offended on the cat's behalf. Nina grabbed her phone off the bedside table and searched the hashtag. The video had been shared thousands of times. Someone posted a screenshot with the caption: *She's all long brown legs and dripping hair. I see you, girl!*

Nina's cheeks were burning when she tossed her

phone onto the mattress beside her. Great! She was a *New York Times* most notable author and a bona fide damsel in distress. Fun times!

He got up and loaded their plates onto the room service tray table. Nina scooted out of bed and took her case of toiletries into the bathroom.

"Hey, Nina," he called after her.

"Yes?"

"I'm going to be the best friend you ever had."

Nina shut bathroom door with a flourish. Cute, clever and overconfident—not at all her type.

# Seven

Julian had hoped to keep a simple routine until things picked up. He planned on staying close to the hotel and out of the spotlight. He intended to fill his days with early workouts, late swims, light meals and hard liquor. But here was Nina, attention-grabbing Nina—a lightning rod of a woman—sleeping on the other side of a pillow partition, her face soft, her long, brown fingers clutching the blanket and strands of black hair stuck to her cheek.

Typically, he was the guy who slipped out of a woman's bed before dawn, so waking up next to Nina felt intimate. The kind of thing you did with a girlfriend. Not that this was a hookup—far from it. She'd made her position clear. There'd been no funny business. Instead, they stayed up swapping funny stories and laughing in the dark as fireworks burst over the mansion and cast a colorful glow through the windows.

He'd made her admit to having looked him up. How else would she have found Rosie's photo of him returning Wasabi? Even Kat had missed it, and she received Google alerts for even the slightest mention of his name. Julian had asked her what had drawn her to writing. She told him about the journals she'd kept since childhood. He recalled how she'd pried the red leather-bound notebook from his hand. Then she asked him to tell her about the time he worked as a valet at the hotel.

"You remembered!" he said, teasing.

"Oh! Just get on with it!"

So he told her about the time that he'd spotted soap opera actor Tony Cash on the same balcony that he and Nina had stood on the night before. She recognized the name of the soap star. "He played a gambler on *Set the World on Fire*."

"That's the one."

He had just started his shift when the actor stepped out to soak up the last rays of sun and the adulation of his fans pressing at the hotel gates. He flashed a smile, waved then turned his back on the growing crowd. Julian was then dispatched to retrieve a Land Rover and ran off with the key jangling in his pocket. Up until that point he had never considered acting. He was no artist. The summer he'd worked building sets for a local theater company in England had convinced him of that. But he was also convinced that the man on the hotel's balcony wasn't setting the world on fire with his acting abilities. If the bar was set that low, couldn't he step over it?

"How did you get your start?" she asked.

"It wasn't easy."

It took leaving Florida for California, sleeping in his car for weeks, forgoing expensive acting classes and at-

tending cheap matinees instead, getting laughed out of
auditions then slowly, eventually, receiving callbacks
and an offer to play the recurring role of a paramedic
on *Riverside Rescue*. It was something. It was a start.

"Ah, Malcolm!" She twisted onto her side, facing
him. "I loved him."

Pride sparked in Julian. "And he loved the ladies."

She laughed. "He sure did!"

And they talked like that well into the night.

Out of habit, he fumbled around for his phone to
check the time, weather and news. The phone rang in
his hand, rousing Nina from sleep. Julian fought the urge
to reach over the pillow partition and soothe her. The last
time he'd touched her without warning, she'd leaped out
of her skin. She was a bit jumpy. He silenced the ringer
but couldn't ignore the call. It was Amelia Chin, long-
time family friend and his former landlady for all of one
week. He'd promised to take her to the orchid market
in Homestead. Was that today? Crap! That was today!

"Hey! Amelia! Good morning." Nina squirmed next
to him and disappeared under the bedspread. Amelia
suggested he pick her up before ten to avoid traffic and
heat and all the rest. "Sounds reasonable. What time is
it now?" Nina slipped out of bed and tiptoed across the
room to the bathroom. Did she think he was talking to
another woman? He was, of course. But Amelia was old
enough to be his grandmother. And it was precisely because she reminded him of his grandmother that he was
taking her out flower shopping. "Eight thirty? I better
get a move on, then. See you soon."

Julian kicked back the sheets and rushed to knock
on the closed door between them. She opened almost

immediately, her toothbrush in her mouth, something hard in her eyes.

"What? No good morning?" he said, teasing. "I saved your life last night."

She pulled the toothbrush out of her mouth. Again, he had to fight the urge to wipe at the smudge of blue toothpaste on her lower lip. "You were on the phone. And how long are you going to keep that up?"

"Until it gets old, and it hasn't yet," he said. "Want to go orchid shopping today?"

She stared at him, confusion marking her sleep-creased face. But she didn't say no.

Julian sent for his car and driver for the trip to Homestead. When it arrived, he waited in the back seat of the Escalade for Nina to come down. Pete, the driver, sat drumming the steering wheel, humming a tune, as the wait dragged on. Julian was just so relieved that she'd said yes that he didn't mind. No question, this outing would be more fun with Nina. They never seemed to run out of things to talk about or, more accurately, to tease and taunt each other about. And the long trip to Homestead promised to be tedious. He loved Amelia, but shopping for orchids wasn't his idea of a good time.

Finally, the gates parted and Nina stepped out in a pair of denim shorts and a cotton halter top, sunglasses on top of her head. Both he and Pete reached for their door handles. "Not so fast," Julian said, stopping him. "This is my job." He sprang out of the black SUV and held the door open for Nina.

"Sorry I kept you waiting. I don't do well with last-minute invitations," she said. "I'm not that spontaneous."

He helped her climb in, taking a moment to admire

the curve of her bottom. She might not want to sleep with him. He could make no such assertion.

"I gave up on you," Julian said, sliding in next to her. "Pete here kept me going."

"Hi, Pete," she said, tugging the seat belt across her torso. "I'm Nina."

"Good morning," he said, and pushed the start engine button. Julian had previously given him the itinerary. They'd make one stop in the neighborhood of El Portal before heading south to Homestead.

Nina arranged her tote bag on her lap then eyed him with suspicion. "Orchids, huh?"

"Okay, you got me," Julian said. "We're location scouting."

She brightened at this. "For a film?"

He nodded. "I need a clear field to land a helicopter. In the scene, I jump out and fight ten men. I take them all out, but a grenade detonates and the helicopter explodes, sending me, or my stunt double, flying. I haven't committed to doing my own stunts this time around."

"Can't you make a movie without explosives?"

"And disappoint my dwindling fan base? Not on your life."

She tucked a lock of hair behind her ear. Today she wore it wavy and loose and still a little damp. He caught a hint of her perfume and wanted to lean close, so he did the opposite, leaning back and folding his arms across his chest.

"Your fans will evolve as you evolve."

"Aren't you a fountain of wisdom this morning! You must have slept well."

"It's the truth," she said. "You deserve the truth."

"And so do you," he said. "We're going to Homestead to shop for orchids. And that's all."

"Okay. But who with?" she asked.

"You and your questions…" he said, mocking.

"Look. I agreed to be your friend, not your wing person."

"Are you always so easily riled up?" he asked. "You really need to work on that."

She bit back a quick response. "You know what? You're right. I'm on vacation. I need to chill."

"You've decided to stay."

"Might as well. What do I have to rush back to?"

"Work," he suggested.

"No." Her shoulders slumped low. "I'm on sabbatical."

He would have liked for her to say more, to open up about her life down to the nitty-gritty, but she clammed up.

"I've been on sabbatical a year," he said.

"That long?" she said. "Is it liberating?"

"It's soul crushing."

"Oh." Her eyes flooded with concern. She blinked a few times and offered him a crooked grin. "Breeding orchids is an interesting choice, but I support you."

"You mock me, but it's a billion-dollar industry."

"Is that a fact?"

"Oh, yeah. Easy money."

Pete cleared his throat, reminding Julian that they were not alone—much as it felt that way. "Traffic is light. The destination is ten minutes away."

Nina leaned forward to ask Pete a question. "What's ten minutes away?"

He glanced at her in the rearview mirror. "It's not for me to say."

"Smart man," Julian said.

"Are you here from California?" Pete asked Nina, expertly changing the subject.

"No such luck," Julian replied.

"We can't all be California girls," Nina said with a sigh.

They arrived at Amelia's house. Pete pulled up to the curb. Nina turned to look out the window, studying the modest yellow house sitting on a generous lot.

"We are at the home of my mother's childhood friend Amelia Chin," Julian said. "They grew up in Jamaica together. Amelia gave me a place to stay when I got off the plane from England and didn't know a soul. So today I'm taking her orchid shopping."

Nina was now studying him. "Julian Knight! I could kiss you, that's so sweet."

He could not stop a foolish grin from spreading. "Please do."

She punched him in the shoulder instead.

"Before you think too highly of me, I'm only doing it for the food. She always cooks my favorite meals after I take her out. You'll see. She'll invite us in for lunch afterward."

"Now *that* makes sense," she said, grinning.

Amelia, not one to wait, had come out of her house and was standing on the sidewalk. Julian hopped out of the car and pulled her into a hug. "What are you doing? I was going to ring your doorbell like a proper gentleman."

"You're no gentleman," Amelia said. Turning to Pete, she said, "And you're parked near the hydrant."

"Leave the man alone," Julian said. "I can afford the ticket."

"You'll get towed! Can you afford the aggravation?"

Amelia looked the same as she did when he last visited, five years earlier. Her fine features were bracketed with deep and fine lines, but she was still as vibrant and energetic.

"All right, then, why are we wasting time? Let's get out of here before the tow truck arrives."

At the orchid market, Nina stayed behind with Pete, allowing Julian and Amelia to wander the stalls alone and catch up for a bit. The market was a field large enough to land a helicopter but dense with palms and bamboo. She leaned against the car and watched him assist the older woman, her frail hand locked in a death grip around his thick forearm. Nina was inexplicably moved.

Pete had gone off to buy refreshments, and he returned with chilled bottles of water. "Mr. Knight says you're an old friend. How far back do you go? Since before he was famous?"

"Not that far back," Nina said.

"I read that he and his girlfriend broke up."

Nina took a sip of water. She didn't like the turn of the conversation. She supposed anyone who'd stood in a supermarket checkout line had read all the details of the Julian and Bettina seismic split. Still, she was not going to discuss it with Pete.

"If you're going to make a move, now is the time."

"Excuse me?"

"Just saying."

Nina went still. Back home in the city, she could silence a chatty cab driver with one sharp glance before things went too far—and things had officially gone too far.

"I think it's time to catch up with Julian and Amelia."

Nina slipped on her dark glasses and marched down the makeshift aisles lined with tables crammed with orchids in various state of bloom. The Florida heat weighed on her shoulders like a damp blanket. She couldn't shake the feeling of being watched and glanced over her shoulder to check on Pete. He was on his phone, his back to her. The feeling persisted. And then she caught it—the flash of a camera.

A photographer was hiding behind a cluster of palms, camera lens pointed at Julian and Amelia. She stiffened with anger, torn between wanting to attack the photographer and rushing over to shield Julian from view. The flash of the camera snapped her out of her inertia. She ran to Julian.

At her approach, he held up a potted orchid with milk-white petals peppered with purple dots and a splash of yellow. "Look what we got."

"It's a Mystic Isle," Amelia said. "My favorite."

"Lovely!" Nina took care to position herself in the photographer's line of sight, obscuring his shot. Under normal circumstances, she would have found this exchange about flowers delightful, but unfortunately some shady paparazzo was documenting every second. She glanced over her shoulder to confirm this, and the flash went off again in the distance.

Nina waited until Amelia was out of earshot to alert Julian, out of fear of rattling the older woman. Even though, to be fair, Amelia did not seem like the type of woman who was easily rattled.

"Listen up," she said. "There's a photographer in the bushes. Twelve o'clock."

Julian wasn't rattled in the least. "I spotted him a while ago, and that's six o'clock. Not twelve."

"Who cares about his coordinates?" Nina snapped. "This is still a gross invasion of privacy."

"I'm used to it," he said. "Did you fly across the field to protect me?"

"I… I…" Irritation and embarrassment clogged Nina's throat. She was not so jaded to shrug off the presence of a lurking photographer.

Julian pinched her cheek. "You're a true friend, Nina."

Amelia returned with two more plants. "I'm done. We should go now. I'll get dizzy in this heat."

Nina was relieved. They didn't have to kick the photographer's ass, but they also didn't have to linger and give him a show.


Paparazzi presence at the orchid field had pissed Julian off—and justifiably so. He'd played it down to reassure Nina, who'd seemed genuinely upset. Plus he hadn't wanted to rattle poor Amelia. As to be expected, Katia wasted no time calling. They were on their way back to the hotel when his phone rang.

"Here's a tweet for you," Kat said. She went on to read it, hashtags and all, adding emphasis wherever needed for drama. "'Shelve this under #shamelessactsofself-promotion: JLK buys a little old lady a bunch of flowers then helps her across the street. Like…really? That's piling it on thick! So now he suddenly respects women? #notbuyingit #RescueMeJLK is a sham.'"

Julian switched the phone from one ear to the other. "Thanks for the update. You don't have to call for every little thing, you know."

"You're wrong!" she exclaimed. "This is major. I love where you're going with this."

"Not going anywhere with anything," Julian said. "I took a family friend on an outing."

"You saved a cat. You saved a drowning girl. You helped a little old lady across the street. See a pattern yet?"

"That's nonsense."

"That's gold! That photo of you kneeling before the little girl is the kind of thing that rehabs an image. You can't buy that kind of publicity."

"Clearly, not everyone is buying it."

"Don't worry about that. We need the naysayers. They're useful."

He looked over to Nina, a potted white orchid on her lap. At some point, she'd gathered her hair in a knot on top of her head. He wished he could snap a picture of her. "Katy Kat, I've got to go."

"Sure, but do me one favor—think up some more heroics. Let's get #RescueMeJLK trending."

"All right. Hanging up now."

He ended the call and tossed the phone from one hand to another, hot potato style.

"Everything okay?" Nina asked.

He'd let her decide. He searched for the tweet and showed it to her.

"Wow, that was fast," she said.

The attached photo showed Julian carrying a cardboard box overflowing with paper-white orchids. Amelia walked beside him, her arm linked around his. Nina walked a step ahead, leading the way. He loved the way she walked—always light on her feet and with those long, sure strides.

He'd helped Amelia carry the flowers to the car, but it was Nina who paid attention to her lengthy instructions on how best to graft an orchid onto a tree. Back at Amelia's house, Nina ate most of the ackee and salt fish that she'd prepared for him. When he protested, she reminded him that he was a vegetarian.

"*Mostly* vegetarian."

"Then you won't mind if I eat *most* of this."

He smiled remembering the afternoon. Just as he'd predicted, Nina had made his day better. Still, she wasn't over the incident.

"Is it normal for paparazzi to follow you around like this?" she asked.

"Not lately."

"Hmm…" She pulled out her own phone and tapped on the screen. *"You're gonna eat those words."*

The words were spoken in Julian's voice, but an octave lower and without a trace of a British accent. The musical score to *Thunder* swelled in the car. Nina turned ashen and stabbed the phone screen with her fingers, desperate to silence it.

Julian let out a shout. Kat, the tweet and the meddlesome paparazzi were forgotten. "Naughty Nina Taylor, what have you been up to? Are you binge-watching me?"

"Don't flatter yourself!" she said. "Thought I'd get familiar with your work. That's all."

"In that case…" He pulled up her audiobook, and her words flowed from his phone. *"My mother played dress up and make-believe for a living. She wore makeup and costumes and performed on stage. We did not go to church. On Sunday mornings, when she wasn't performing, we attended matinees."*

"Oh, God, no!"

She ripped off her seat belt and lunged forward to wrestle the phone from his hand. He let her exhaust herself awhile, holding his phone out of her reach, just to enjoy the feel of her body. Her top might as well have been cut out of tissue paper. He felt everything, and everything felt wonderful. Her round breasts crushed against his chest, her bare thigh slid against his.

"Settle down," he murmured in her ear. "And buckle up. Safety first."

She moved away from him, her cheeks flushed. When she was settled, she returned her attention to the orchid, the only near casualty of their tussle. A long time passed before she spoke up. "I don't think you play make-believe for a living. I have a lot of respect for the profession."

Warmth spread through Julian's chest. "I knew that," he said. Although it was good to hear her say it.

"In those early journals, I'm such a brat," she said. "I went on and on about how horrible it was to be the daughter of a struggling actress. Only it wasn't so bad. It was special and unique, and I wouldn't trade it for some cookie-cutter upbringing in the suburbs."

"Did your mother have a chance to read it?" he asked.

She let out a bitter laugh. "I don't have to tell you that she hated it. She thought it tarnished her image, and she's probably right. Then she died before I got a chance to publish anything else. Now my publisher wants another memoir, and I can't bring myself to do it."

Julian wished they could get to the hugging stage of this relationship, because he desperately wanted to pull her close. "Hey, listen," he said. "Your mother wasn't objective. You do a good job showing her humanity."

"She didn't want to be human, Julian. She wanted to be a star."

"Stars burn out."

She turned to him, eyes brimming with questions.

Good thing Pete pulled up to the gates of Sand Castle. Julian helped Nina step out of the car, hyperaware of the glances and phones angled their way. He rested a hand on the small of her back and ushered her up the stone steps and into the courtyard, heading toward the lift.

"I smell like a horse," he said, close to her ear. "Shopping for flowers is hard work."

"I smell like roses," she said.

"Of course."

"But I'm grimy," she admitted.

"I'll race you to the shower."

"You can have the shower," she said. "I want to soak in a bath."

The front desk clerk chased them down. "Ms. Taylor! Wait! There's news!"

Nina turned to him expectantly. Julian had a feeling that he wouldn't like the news. When the doors to the lift parted, he wanted to stuff Nina inside.

"Your room will be available in the morning. I wanted to tell you myself."

Nina cleared her throat. "That's great. Thanks."

On the ride up, her mood flattened. She stood fussing with the plant.

Julian leaned against the back wall. "If this is going to be our last night as roommates, maybe we should order in."

She looked up at him. The spark had returned. "I'd like that."

# Eight

Nina woke up alone in the large bed. The note on the pillow beside her was short. *Morning workout—J.*

The night before, she and Julian had stayed up late. He'd recommended they watch *Thunder* on a large screen in high definition and with surround sound. "It's not the type of movie you can watch on your phone."

They ordered dinner, tossed silk pillows and a blanket onto the antique rug, and camped out on the bedroom floor. They watched the movie, and when the credits rolled, Nina grabbed the remote control and hit Pause.

"Straight talk?"

"Absolutely."

"It's not trash."

"Think so?" He stretched out on the pillows. "That's a three-star review in my book."

"And you're hot in it," she said. "Really, really hot."

His eyes flashed. "Are you trying to start something tonight?"

"Only a conversation," she said. Although she couldn't deny that being this close to him sent waves of warmth through her body. "Ever heard of the Bechdel test? Two named female characters in a film discuss something—anything—other than a man."

"I've heard of it. I'm not a caveman," he said. "And I know it doesn't apply here."

"How could it? None of your female characters have names." Nina pointed to the screen frozen on the list of characters by order of appearance. "Girl in Yellow Bikini... Ferrari Girl... Casino Girl Number One... Casino Girl Number Two... Girl at the Bar... All you're missing is the Girl with the Dragon Tattoo!"

Julian doubled over with laughter. His T-shirt bunched up to reveal a patch of taut brown skin. Nina sat on her hands to keep from reaching out and discovering more.

"Now repeat after me," she said. "Representation matters!"

"Don't blame me. I had no say in the matter."

"But you were the star!"

Nina would not let him off the hook. Some actors had inclusion clauses in their contracts to improve representation of women and minorities on film sets.

"I got the job because I looked the part," he said. "If I made noise, they'd have kicked me off the project. I was no one and I had zero clout. I got that job on my headshot alone."

"Really?"

He winked. "It was a good headshot."

Such a modest man! "Okay, but later—"

"Later, the criticism caught up with them. That's when they brought in Bettina to play a computer scientist."

Nina reached for her glass of wine and took a swallow. "And that's where they went wrong. The one woman with any agency is a computer scientist in a film populated with assassins and criminal masterminds. What's lacking is a female crime lord, assassin, bomb expert... You know...the type of character that is central to the plot."

His expression clouded over, and Nina knew she'd touched on something. "Aha! I love it when I'm right!"

He reached out and brushed a lock of hair from her cheek in a surprisingly tender gesture. "What do you love about it? The ego boost?"

"Maybe," Nina replied in a whisper. "You may not be the only egomaniac at the Sand Castle."

They'd stayed up late, talking. But in the morning, she awoke in bed, on her side of the pillow partition, with no idea on how she'd gotten there.

The lines were blurring fast.

"We serve breakfast anywhere. Our guests love to lounge by the pool."

"Where would I go if I wanted to avoid the guests?"

"The rooftop deck is deserted at this hour."

"So that's where I'll be."

Nina took a stack of magazines up to the roof. An attendant promptly brought her a mimosa and a platter of fruit. She took a seat at an umbrella table with a view of the pool. Just as she got settled, her phone chimed with a text message.

Hey there! Just checking in.

It was her cousin Valerie Pierre. She never checked in; they weren't close. Valerie was the one relative on her father's side whose contact information she'd bothered to save. Nina's parents were only together long enough to conceive her. They were two New Jersey kids who met, predictably enough, at a party in the city. Her mother was the aspiring actress who'd caught the acting bug from performing in church. Her father was the son of practical-minded Haitian immigrants, who dreamed of writing poetry. Nina's mother had never encouraged her writing; it was the one obvious trait she'd inherited from her father.

The timing of the text was suspect. Her cousin lived somewhere in South Florida—that much Nina knew. If she'd kept up with celebrity gossip this past weekend, it was possible that she'd spotted Nina in a viral video or two.

*Enough! Just answer the message!*

Nina had the terrible habit of overthinking everything. It was just a text, and Valerie had always been friendly. Nina thought of an appropriate answer and riddled it with exclamation points. Hey there! All is good!! Happy holiday weekend!!!

The response came quick.

I know it's a difficult time for you… With the anniversary and all.

Nina read the message a few times. It was possible that her cousin was checking in out of sincere concern. Why hadn't she considered that? Her eyes glazed with tears as she punched a response. Yes… Thank you.

Of course! We're family. Call me whenever. Okay?

Nina set the phone aside and gazed down at the pool, seeing it for the first time without the hordes of partygoers. The word *pool* was deceptive, evoking the smoke of coal barbecues, overcooked burgers and cheap beer. This wasn't so much a pool but *the* fountain of youth hidden in a garden of tropical flowers. The morning sun beat down on the diamond-clear surface. The surrounding grounds were immaculate. Grassy patches were cut into geometric shapes and laid out like stained glass. Where vegetation lacked it was hand-painted onto the walls. A half a dozen guests were lounging half-naked on sun beds, working off hangovers or working on their tans. The men came in all shapes, colors and sizes. The women were uniformly slim. They offered their bikini-clad bodies to the sun but kept their faces hidden under wide-brimmed hats. There were no kids among them. Sand Castle had a no-child policy, solidifying its reputation as an adult playground.

Nina hummed a tune. *Heaven. I'm in heaven.*

A man peeled himself off a bed and made his way to the edge of the pool. He dived in and swam a lap in slow, smooth strokes. He moved freely, as if he didn't feel the weight of the eyes pinned on him, and climbed out the other end. Water swirled down his broad back and golden-brown limbs.

Something short-circuited in Nina's mind.

She got up from the table, approached the deck rail and watched, transfixed, as Julian grabbed a towel off the back of a chair and wiped himself down. He dropped the rumpled towel in a basket and stood still a moment, hands on narrow hips, head back, face offered to the sun.

~~Heaven.~~ *I'm in hell.*

Nina's breath went shallow as need and want coiled inside her. She ran through the *not my type* argument one more time. Some women preferred men who could change a flat tire or handle power tools. Nina didn't own a car, plus she had a competent handyman on speed dial. She liked brainy guys, the type who could review her tax returns, give her investment advice or draft a cease-and-desist letter in a pinch. Practical stuff. And there was one more thing: she didn't date actors. Never had. Never would. She had a lot of respect for the profession; that was the truth. To get sucked into that world again, all that drama, she'd sooner jump out of a plane just for kicks. But Julian... Oh, God, Julian... Was he worth it? Was she overthinking it? Their future together was capped to the five nights she had left on this vacation. Then it was back home to a life that did not include buff movie stars splashing around in pools.

Now the buff actor was staring up at her, grinning and waving, doing his best to grab her attention. It was cute because he didn't have to work so hard. He had all her attention, all the time.

Moments later, he joined her on the deck. She stood and smoothed down her linen shirtdress.

"Don't move," he said. "Sit."

She eased back into the chair and watched him drop his gym bag to the ground, pull out a camera and raise it to his eyes. "What are you doing?"

"You are so beautiful in the morning. I want you to see what I see."

Nina laughed off the extravagant compliment. While he snapped a few photos, she lost herself, watching him. He had a healthy post-workout glow. He wore a loose T-shirt, but his muscles were taut and glistening from his swim.

"Sit down. I ordered breakfast," she said. "Want anything?"

"I'll grab a protein shake," he said.

"Of course you will."

"Believe it or not," he said, "maintaining this body requires discipline and sacrifice."

Julian was not as bulky as in his films. She imagined that physique required months of intense training to achieve and the discipline of a pro wrestler to maintain. He kept to a strict diet and workout regime. As a result, he was lean and toned to an inch of his life. Generally, Nina avoided this type of guy, jocks and gym rats and the like. She wanted her man fit but miraculously so. Maybe he played ball with his friends on weekends. Maybe he built muscle chopping firewood or whatnot. Either way, he ate real food, didn't obsess over protein powders or stock up on power bars.

That was before she met Julian.

The rooftop attendant arrived with her food. She'd selected the Cuban breakfast, consisting of scrambled eggs, sliced avocado, *pico de gallo* and crusty bread. Julian eyed her plate lustfully. Still, he ordered a protein shake with added greens.

"Any preference of greens, Mr. Knight?"

"No preference. Just toss everything in."

"Yes, Mr. Knight."

"Mmm." Nina patted her belly. "Sounds delicious."

He flashed a smile, displaying a row of perfect white teeth. "Don't mock me, Nina."

She grabbed her fork and loaded it with eggs and avocado. "Try this," she said, holding it up to his lips.

"Don't tempt me, Nina," he said. "I'm trying to be good."

"Come on, Julian," she whispered. "Live a little. I won't tell your personal trainer."

He locked eyes with her. Then he took the fork in his mouth, his teeth scraping the prongs as he pulled away. The desire to kiss him was so sharp it cut her appetite.

She dropped the fork and picked up the bread. She ripped a piece and bit into it, buying some time. It was light and chewy and delicious. "I work out and eat right and all the things," she said. "Just not on vacation. It's against my religion to be so disciplined at a five-star hotel."

He relaxed in his chair and stretched out his legs, brown skin over taut muscle. "What church is that? Can I convert?"

"Sorry. We only let in true believers."

The attendant returned with his shake, topped off Nina's mimosa with champagne, then discreetly backed away.

Julian stirred the thick shake with a glass straw. "I'm going to miss you tonight."

Those few words undid her. She cleared her throat. "How about we continue our marathon with *Thunder II*?"

"You've been through enough," he said. "Plus, I have a thing tonight."

"Oh!" She had to grip the bread or risk dropping it. "I… Oh."

Of course he had a thing—whatever that meant. He hadn't flown across country to swim laps in a fancy pool. Unlike her, he had a life. Nina scarfed down her eggs, aware that he was watching her. He was such a keen observer. Nothing was lost on him. She'd pay cash to know what he was thinking.

"It's a work thing," he said. "The last time I met with this person, we spoke for hours. I have no idea how it will go tonight, but I'm hopeful."

She reached for her glass and raised it. "Good luck."

"Thanks." He continued to stir his shake, in no apparent hurry to drink it. "What are your plans for today?"

"There's the move to my new room, and that'll take all of ten minutes."

He offered to help, and she turned him down. "I'm good. Thanks."

"What else?"

At this point, she should initiate plan WWMD: What would Mom do? "The point of this trip is to celebrate my mother's life. So I'm going to do the things that she'd like to do, given the chance."

"Which are?"

"Lounging at this fabulous hotel, drinking, flipping through magazines… I'll have to book a manicure." She shrugged, failing to come up with anything better. "She took relaxation very seriously."

"What are the things that you like to do?"

"Me?" Why had the question stumped her? "Honestly, I don't vacation well. I work a lot of the time. So I'd read or revise a manuscript or use the trip to research a setting."

The straw clinked on the sides of his glass as he continued to stir. He was mulling over something. Nina held her breath until he came out with it.

"Why don't you come with me tonight?" he said.

"To the work thing?"

"It's a dinner."

"I don't know," she said, suddenly uneasy.

"You might enjoy it. And you'd be doing me a favor—I'm the third wheel."

Nina immediately considered what she might wear and missed it when he lifted his gym bag onto his lap. He pulled out his phone. "What's your email address?"

"Why?"

"I'm going to send you some reading materials," he said. "You might want to study up for tonight."

"Oh? Okay," she said. "Send it to *Hello@NinaTaylor.com*."

He narrowed his eyes, tapping away at his phone. "I don't have to remind you that anything I share with you is confidential."

"Should I remind you that friendship is based on trust?"

He put the phone down. "Is that what this is? A platonic friendship?"

"I don't know what this is," she said. And that was the honest truth.

He seemed to like her answer. Concealing a smile, he drew the straw from the shake, set it down on a napkin and drained the glass with a few gulps. His Adam's apple bobbed when he swallowed.

Nina's mouth went dry.

He rose to his feet. "I need a shower."

"What time is dinner?" she asked.

"Seven. I'll come get you."

"See you then."

He turned to walk away, hesitated, then returned to his seat. "Nina, I'm nearly done with your book."

She groaned. He raised a finger. "Let me say this one thing. You don't have far to go to connect with your mum. You saw her clearly for who she was, and that's a lot."

Nina shook her head, regret and sorrow churning in her gut. "She didn't see it that way."

Her mother had read an early excerpt of *Backstage Diva*. She wept and accused Nina of distorting facts to paint herself in a positive light.

"Why do you think I insist that you, that everyone, call me Julian?" he said.

"It's a beautiful name," she said.

"Most people can't separate me from the person they see on screen. It's annoying, for one thing. And it's isolating."

"Oh, Julian…" The name escaped her lips, now full of meaning.

"You were not her *fan*. You were her daughter. She had something real with you, and it's a shame she couldn't see it."

He got up and slung his gym bag over his shoulder. Nina watched him leave, speechless. Every time she thought she had this man figured out, he revealed another facet of himself. Curiosity as to what he might have sent her in the email took over. She grabbed her phone and clicked on the message. The attached document was titled *Midnight Sun*.

Nina finished her breakfast and took her drink over to a lounge chair. It was time to hit Pause on plan WWMD. She had a fresh drink and new reading material. This was *her* idea of fun.

# Nine

Julian stood at Nina's door in a steel-gray suit that his stylist had had delivered after he put in an emergency call. He'd wanted to look good for their night out, only they were staying in. Francisco had agreed to meet at Sand Castle. Actually, he'd insisted on it.

Nina looked stunning in what couldn't be dismissed as a little black dress, because the long bias-cut skirt had a high slit and the bodice was completely backless. Julian went stiff with want. He yearned to take her in his arms, and it took effort to suppress the urge.

"Don't just stand there," she said. "Come in! I have something for you."

He stepped into her room and cast a look around. The Garden Room lived up to its name with hand-painted flowers scattered all over the walls, a bed covered with a floral duvet and drapes with stitched flowers framing a view of the enclosed garden—the one with the famed statue of Aphrodite. As an added touch, the orchid Amelia had selected for her was sitting on the nightstand. "So, this is it," he said. "Like it?"

"I like it well enough." She walked to a corner desk and grabbed a few sheets of paper. "I read the screenplay and made notes."

Julian took the few pieces of hotel stationery from her hands and inspected them. "I should've thought twice before asking a writer to read anything."

She snatched the pages from him. "It's a good thing. I'm excited!"

"But are you hungry?" he asked, hoping for a diversion. "Ready for dinner?"

"Ready! I'll grab my purse."

She headed over to the dresser and dabbed perfume on the insides of her wrists. The gesture was so intimate, Julian felt privileged to watch it.

"Nina," he said.

She tossed him a look over her shoulder. He forgot what he wanted to say.

"Yes?"

"Uh… Right. Bring your notes. It's early. We can talk over drinks."

"Ah!" She folded the pages into a tiny clutch purse. "Now you're talking my love language."

They were seated at the hotel bar with a half hour ahead of them. When Francisco and his date arrived, they'd have the dining room to themselves—Julian had seen to it. Who knew how many first dates and birthday dinners were canceled to accommodate him? Only he wasn't too worried about it, not if it meant guaranteeing quiet time with Nina…and Francisco, too.

Their reflection was splashed against the mirrored wall. Seated like this, facing each other, dressed as they were, Julian couldn't deny it: they were one *smoking*-hot couple. Not that appearances mattered for anything. Still, it was hard to ignore the truth.

Hands shaking, she pulled her notes from her bag and smoothed them on the onyx bar top. "You wrote *Midnight Sun*," Nina said. "There's nothing you can say to convince me otherwise."

He paused, took a sip of his gin and tonic. "What makes you say that?"

Julian had taken precautions to send her an unmarked copy. He'd wanted her honest opinion.

"Every character sounds like you," she said.

He winced and reached for his drink again.

"Don't look so worried. I told you I liked it."

He thumbed through her notes open on the onyx bar top. "So, what's all this?"

"Just some notes." She sat up straight and crossed her legs. The slit of the skirt spread to reveal toned thighs. Julian's gaze skidded off the pages onto her lap. "Which role are you playing?"

Julian hesitated. Would she be disappointed when he told her? He wasn't the star of his own movie. He couldn't be. If he were going to salvage his career, he'd have to try new things. And he couldn't do that if a film's success rested on his name and image. That left him with supporting roles, which meant his star would dim. Not the one on Hollywood Boulevard, thankfully. That one was set in concrete.

"I play Luke."

"The con artist? Oh, God… I love him!"

In that moment, Julian loved her.

"That scene when he drives Amanda home from the party is so tender," she said. "I'm glad the lead is a woman. That was a good choice."

"Is the dialogue *that* terrible?"

"Actors need lines. Good delivery isn't enough. It has to be on the page. I learned that from my mother."

She was so brilliant; Julian couldn't get over it. When she picked up her dirty martini, he reached out and toyed with the gold bracelet at her wrist. She brought the glass to her lips, her eyes on him, her expression dark. If he didn't know better, he'd swear that she was making up her mind about him. God, he liked his chances!

"Julian! There you are!"

Francisco was early. Nina turned to the voice and recognized the actor. In his motorized chair, he looked sharp in a dark blue suit. She slipped off the bar stool and floated over to him. "Francisco Cortes! What an honor!"

Frank beamed up at her. He had not lost his matinee-idol looks: deep tan, chiseled jaw, trim beard and sterling silver hair. Julian approached and introduced her properly. "Frank, this is Nina Taylor. Nina is a very talented writer and a friend."

"Nina, I'm familiar with your work."

"Really?"

She seemed completely flabbergasted. Did she not understand the reach and importance of her work?

"Oh, yes," Frank said. "I caught your mother on stage once. Brilliant performance! And you know we actors love to read about ourselves. That can't be helped."

"Well, I loved you in *The Longest Day*. That might be my favorite movie of all time."

Francisco laughed. "Have I interrupted something? I arrived early, I know."

"Don't be ridiculous," Julian said. "You honor us."

Grace joined them. She and Francisco went way back, and she was his date for the evening. They took off ahead of them, Grace leading the way to the dining room. Nina and Julian followed.

"You weren't that excited to meet me," Julian said, speaking low so only Nina would hear. The added precaution wasn't necessary. Frank and Grace were enthralled with each other.

Nina did nothing to conceal her joy at his petty display of jealousy. "Francisco Cortes isn't disrupting my vacation plans."

"You didn't know any of my films."

"None of your films were featured at the Tribeca Film Festival," she said. "I can't be blamed for that."

"Is Grace single?" he asked. "See how Frank is looking at her?"

"Lucky woman!" Nina exclaimed.

"Go on and twist the knife," he said.

She laughed and slipped her hand in his.

The dining room was an intimate setting with sloped ceilings and shell-inlaid walls that gleamed in flickering candlelight. He'd seen it earlier in the day. Tonight, he had the pleasure of seeing it through Nina's wide eyes. She never held back, and he loved that about her.

A grand table was set for four. After a pleasant meal, Grace left them to talk business. Frank got straight to it.

"I'd like to talk about the script. It needs tightening up."

"Let me guess," Julian said. "The dialogue."

"Bingo!" Frank said with a snap of his fingers. "That

gives me such hope. I thought you were going to give me a hard time."

"It's too late for that. Nina beat you to the punch."

Francisco turned to Nina. "You agree?"

"It needs some dusting up. Otherwise, it's perfect."

No…she was perfect. Her support meant even more to him than she could imagine.

"So, you've agreed to take on a rewrite?" Frank asked.

"Me? No!" Nina looked to Julian in panic. "I'm not a screenplay writer. You know that, right?"

"But you're a writer," Julian said.

"And a damn fine one," Frank added.

"Yes, but— Thanks, but— No."

Julian hoped she didn't feel ambushed. That wasn't his intention. He hadn't thought the script needed any help, but he wasn't so stubborn to refuse it. Why take their chances with a script doctor? Nina would be perfect for the job.

"Welcome to Hollywood," Frank said to her. "Nobody knows anything and we're all just winging it."

Julian couldn't dispute that. If he'd waited around for someone to proclaim him an actor, he would have never had the balls to audition for any role.

"I'll give you my notes. How about that?"

Julian studied her for a while. She was blinking so fast, it was certainly to hold back tears. What could be holding her back? She'd claimed to be excited about the project. All at once, the pieces snapped together in Julian's mind. Why would she want to work with him? She was a respected artist. His legacy was synonymous with mud. With that realization blooming inside him, he turned away from her.

"We'll leave it at that," Frank said. "You must be busy, working on other projects."

"If you don't mind," Nina said, rising to her feet. "I'm going to the ladies' room."

Julian immediately stood to help her with her chair. She rested a hand on his arm and eased him back into his seat. "I'll be right back."

He watched her go. It took a while for him to notice that Frank was staring at him. "God help you, my man! You're in love with that woman."

"No way!" Julian protested. "We've only just met."

"What difference does that make?" Frank asked.

Julian pushed away his dessert plate. "What's going on with you and Grace? Is that love?"

"Maybe? Who knows?"

"You ought to." Frank seemed to know enough to comment on his state of affairs. Shouldn't he be more self-aware?

"Here's what I know," Frank said. "Do the work, find someone to clean up the script and I'll direct. But I have one other request."

Julian was at the edge of his seat. All this talk of love had derailed him. This was the conversation he wanted to have with Frank. "I'm listening."

"You assist me in every way. When we wrap this thing up, I want you to have the tools and know-how to do this on your own. No more shopping around for someone to direct the thing that you've conceived in your imagination. I understand that you need a push, a pat on the back, someone to believe in you, and I'm willing to step into the role. And it's exciting. I'll admit it. But after this, I'm done. And you've got a career ahead of you. *Comprende?*"

"Understood!"

So this was what paying it forward looked and felt like? If so, he'd have to give it a go, because it felt damn good. He reached across the table and shook Frank's hand. "Thanks, man. I don't know what else to say."

"Say you're ready to get to work. I don't believe in wasting time."

Julian was more than ready. And all he had was time.

# Ten

Nina locked herself in the ladies' room. With the scent of lavender swirling in the air and a gold toilet, it was as good a place as any for a meltdown. She lowered the toilet seat and sat down.

Why had she turned down such an awesome opportunity? She loved the material and had great ideas on how to improve it. Julian was open to criticism, which meant he'd be easy enough to work with. Plus, he really needed the help. Over dinner, she'd noticed how nervous he was. Francisco's opinion mattered to him. It wasn't every day that she got the chance to collaborate with people so committed to their work. Lastly, she needed the work. Her inbox wasn't exactly crammed with offers. What was holding her back?

Her agent was going to kill her if she ever found out.

"Nina? Are you in there?"

It was Julian. How long had she been spinning her wheels in this restroom? Long enough that Julian had had to lead a search party. She strained to make her voice chipper. "I'll be right out!"

"What are you doing in there?" His voice was low and muffled, as if he were speaking into the thickness of the door.

"What do you think?" To make her point, she stood and flushed the toilet that didn't need flushing.

"I don't know," Julian said. "My guess is that you're breathing into a paper bag."

Nina did not gratify him with a response. Having flushed, she made a production of washing her hands, splashing water.

His next guess wasn't any better. "Crying into a towel?"

"Oh, God!"

She twisted the gold faucets shut, dried her hands and yanked open the bathroom door. Julian was leaning against the frame. His relaxed posture suggested that he would have waited there all night. And he was so handsome. All that muscle fitted in an immaculate suit. All that smooth brown skin, turned golden by his time in the sun. All the sparkle and intensity in those endless brown eyes. She could barely stand it.

"I'm not having a panic attack, if that's what you're thinking."

"Good," he said. "May I come in?"

This request coming from anyone else would have been bizarre. For whatever reason, she and Julian had skipped the awkward getting-to-know-you phase and were at the point of holding secret meetings in public restrooms.

"Did you leave Francisco alone at the table?" Nina asked.

"He's gone," he said. "He called it a night."

Nina stepped aside and let him in. The generous restroom contracted in size. She eased down onto a tufted bench under a gold-framed mirror. He stood before her, looking down at her upturned face with concern. Why did she feel so exposed in his gaze?

"Julian, I'm okay. Really." She sat up straighter. "I wasn't expecting your offer, that's all."

"I'm sorry," he said. "I shouldn't have assumed you'd want to work with me."

"What do you mean by that?"

His face was clouded. "Like you said, it's not your area of expertise."

For whatever reason, Nina didn't believe his explanation. Julian was holding back from her, and the feeling disturbed her more than was reasonable. "Why wouldn't I want to work with you? You're a big Hollywood star."

"I'm a big liability."

"Julian!" Nina rose to confront him. "What are you talking about? I'd love to work with you."

"Because you split your time between libraries and film festivals, you may not know that my reputation isn't the best."

"I don't split my time—" Nina paused, took a breath. "And you're being dramatic. So your movie tanked. So what?"

"It's not just that."

"I know," Nina said, waving her hands to brush the whole ugly business away. "There was a boycott and everything. And I'm sure you're not blameless, but you are not who those people say you are. You're not."

Emotion colored his face, prompting Nina to wonder about Julian's carefree facade.

"Then why were you so quick to say no?"

"Because I suck at fiction!" Julian pushed out a dry laugh. She grabbed his shoulders to force him to listen. "I've been writing all my life, and the memoir is my only successful project. My editor turned down a collection of short stories just this week. I'd feel more comfortable if you hired a professional to do this job."

He removed her hands from his shoulders and held them between his. "Would a professional care as much as you do?"

"Who cares? Nothing is better than competence."

Julian's voice was level. "I care a great deal."

They stood like that for a long time, her hands in his, their eyes locked. Julian's quiet confidence transferred onto her. Turning him down was the sensible thing to do, but would she regret it? Yes. Yes, she would. Certainty surged inside her. She was going to do it. She was going to jump into the deep. Only this time she was fully aware of the risk.

"Okay. I'll do it."

Julian asked her to repeat her words, as if he couldn't believe what he'd just heard.

"I'll do it," Nina said. "I'll take a chance. So long as you keep in mind that I've never done this type of work before."

"You're in good company," he said. "Neither have I. But if you want to come aboard this sinking ship, I'll be more than happy to have you."

Nina planted her hands on her hips. "Permission to come aboard, sailor."

"Permission granted."

He flashed a grin so infectious that she couldn't help but grin back. And then she snapped out of it. This was a negotiation, damn it! "I don't work for free."

"I wouldn't expect you to," Julian said.

"My agent will be in touch."

"We'll work something out," he said. "You won't be disappointed."

"One last thing," she said. "If at any point you're not happy with my work, please let me know."

"I'll be straightforward with you," he said. "But unhappy? I don't see it."

"Okay…" Nina said. What was left to cover?

"Now would be a good time to tell you that Frank signed on to be our director."

"Julian!" Nina bolted forward to draw him into an ungainly hug. "That's great! I'm so excited for you."

"For us." He held her close. "He's your director, too."

His breath fanned her cheek. Nina pulled back to look up at him. Those deep brown eyes… That flared nose… Those full lips… All within reach. *I'll do it. I'll take a chance.* As tall as she stood in her heels, she was not tall enough. She placed her hands on his shoulders one more time and, eyes half-closed, she tilted her head back, asking, *imploring*, for a kiss.

The kiss never came.

There was a knock on the door. Nina sprang away from him. If they were caught together in a public bathroom, social media would go nuts. Julian brought a finger to his lips and gestured for her to be quiet.

"Busy here!" he called out in a smooth voice.

A woman's steely tone drilled through the door. "Sir, this is the ladies' room!"

"You might want to rethink your gender norms, ma'am!"

An indignant cry, the staccato click-clack of heels, then blissful silence. Nina collapsed with laughter. Good thing Julian was there to catch her.

"I bet she's headed straight to the complaint desk," he said.

"With good reason. You shamed her and called her ma'am!"

"I'll step out first," he said. "Come find me in the courtyard."

The courtyard was dark except for the light from a few lanterns and a silver disk of a moon. Nina found Julian walking in circles, pausing only to smooth back his hair. When he saw her, he straightened his shoulders and pasted a smile on his face. Nina wasn't duped. Why did he look so conflicted?

Once she'd decided that she wanted him, she hadn't stopped to consider whether the feeling was mutual. Did he…not want this? Nina could address the matter in a straightforward way. Yet she opted to play coy instead. Because that always worked. "Hey," she said, taking a step forward. "We have a few things to celebrate tonight. Let's order champagne."

"Did you want me to kiss you in there?"

Oh, God! Why couldn't he let her play coy? "Yeah… about that… Did you not want to?"

"I had to be sure," he said. "You remember saying you didn't want to sleep with me, right?"

"When did I say that?"

"The first night we slept together—or shared a bed, I should say."

"Oh?" Nina replayed the tape in her mind. He couldn't hold that against her! She was bent out of shape that night. "Nothing after drowning really counts."

"Nina, I'm the mistake women make after a few drinks at a party. I don't want to be something you regret."

"That's not possible."

"Kiss My Ass" video notwithstanding, he was a good person. No amount of mean tweets and mean-spirited magazine articles was going to change her opinion of him. He was the man who dived into a pool, fully dressed, to rescue her after she'd spent the afternoon tossing back vodka shots. That man was the real MVP.

"I'm the woman who has never taken a guy home after a couple of drinks. Not ever." He arched his brows as though impressed. She immediately set him straight. "I don't say this to brag. It's not fun. I overthink and overanalyze everything and everyone."

"So, what's your take on us?"

"Well…here I am in Miami, in this gorgeous mansion. By some strange twist of fate, I met a man. He makes me feel like a goddess, but I wish he'd stop treating me like one, because I'm ready to be reckless and toss caution out the stained glass windows."

His grin broke like the dawn of a new day. "I'm your guy. Reckless behavior is my specialty."

Nina rushed to him, grabbed him by the lapel of his exquisite blazer and drew his mouth to hers. This time, he crushed her with his kiss. She reciprocated, exploring his mouth, taking his moans deep into her own. As the night breeze brushed her bare back, Nina was reminded of where they were: out in the open, perilously exposed. That feeling of being watched returned, and it was all but confirmed by the sound of footsteps in the courtyard. Julian didn't miss it, either. He groaned in frustration and pulled away to look around. Nina shivered, already missing his touch. She froze when she heard him say, "Hey there, Pete. Still on the clock?"

Pete! Why was he lurking around?

"On my way out, Mr. Knight," the driver replied. "Good evening, Ms. Taylor."

"Good night, Pete."

Nina grabbed Julian's arm and led him along the shadows of the cloisters toward the elevator. They passed the door to the bell tower. Julian pushed on the iron handle, and the heavy wood door swung open to a narrow stairwell with steep steps winding up to the top. Nina shot him a warning look. "Not in these shoes."

He glanced down at her delicate heels. "Thought you were ready to be reckless."

"I did say that, didn't I?"

Julian drew her into the stairwell and shut the door behind them. He hunched low before her and ran his hands along her calves. His fingers found and worked diligently to loosen the many buckles and straps of her sandals. Then he eased them off and tossed them aside. When he was done, he looked up at her. "Race you to the top."

"I don't think—"

He charged the stairs before she could dissuade him.

"Hey!" Nina cried. Her competitive nature kicked in, and she might have caught up to him if she hadn't stopped to gather her shoes before giving chase, then stopped midway to catch her breath. Julian stood waiting at the top of the stairs, hands in his pockets, a slice of moonlight adding extra sparkle to his cocky smile.

She glared at him, and he laughed—the laugh of a man who had everything going for him. Nina vowed that he would have the absolute best sex of his life tonight.

"Come on," he said. "You're not dizzy, are you?"

"I'm fine. Thanks." Nina reached the landing and, panting still, ignored his outstretched hand. She stole a moment to take in her surroundings—a circular space with a bleached wood floor and a steepled ceiling. The metal bell swung from an arch facing the courtyard. A built-in bench hugged the walls.

"It's so beautiful," she said, in a whisper.

"Absolutely." He came to stand behind her. "But there's a chance we may be admiring different views."

He swept her braid away from her neck and pressed his lips on each knot of her spine. Her back to Julian's chest, she shivered in his arms. He threaded a hand through the slit of her dress and brushed her inner thigh. She covered his hands with hers and inched it higher. When his fingers brushed between her legs, meeting the wet silky fabric, Nina's back arched, and a moan escaped her. He cupped her face and drew her back for a deeper, more intimate kiss before pulling back.

"Here's my dilemma," he said, speaking softly. "I want to take you up to bed *and* I want to take you right here."

Those options were not mutually exclusive as far as Nina was concerned. She swiveled around to face him. "Can't you do both?"

"Sorry." He kissed the corner of her mouth. "I hate to disappoint, but I'm not prepared."

"Is that all?"

Nina slipped out of his embrace and searched around in the semidarkness for where she might have dropped her small purse. It was clear across the floor. She picked it up and pulled out a square foil packet from the zippered pocket. "Problem solved."

He smiled wickedly. "If you were hoping to get lucky tonight, I hope it was with me."

"Don't flatter yourself. I've kept one in every purse since college."

"I love a girl with a plan."

She made her way back to him on tiptoe, holding up the packet within two fingers. "Women have plans. Girls have hopes and wishes."

Julian's expression darkened as he focused on her. "Scrap your plans. Tell me what you wish for."

That was easy. She didn't have to mull it over. She had wanted to see him naked from the day they'd met. "Take your clothes off."

He took her hand and brought her wrist to his lips. "Please and thank you go a long way, Nina."

"All right," she said, her pulse skipping. "Take your clothes off, *please.*"

Julian shrugged out of his impeccable dinner jacket and started working on the buttons of his shirt. She watched as the layers came off, revealing the broad shoulders, the narrow waist, the ripples of his abdomen and the sculpted thighs. He worked hard at maintaining his body and ought to be lavished with praise and adulation for it. Only Nina was limited and could only offer sarcasm. .

"Wow!" she exclaimed when his boxers joined the heap of clothing. "It doesn't take much to get you naked, JL."

"I believe the words you're searching for are *thank you.*"

Nina wrapped her arms around his neck and whispered her thanks in his ear.

"Now," he said. "One good turn deserves another."

If she had one wish remaining, it would be for her dress to miraculously fall away. Caught up in his kiss, she fumbled with the mini buttons and searched around for the zipper. Julian broke away abruptly. "Oh, for God's sake, woman!"

His hands went straight to a hidden zipper of the skirt. It was as if the man had studied the pattern of her dress all night. With a few adept moves, he had it rising over her head. Then he stood back, his gaze sweeping over her body. She was all but naked except for a pair of fine silk panties. The ocean breeze on her hot skin raised goose bumps. "So bloody beautiful," he murmured before scooping her up and laying her on the banquette.

Somehow, in the tight space, they managed to remain intertwined, kissing, touching, exploring. Nina had never craved anyone's touch as much as his. When she could not take a second longer, Nina took his face in her hands. Between harsh intakes of breaths, she said, "Let's just…do this fast…and…take our time later…upstairs."

He raised himself on an elbow and looked down at her, his eyes teasing. "A woman with a plan…"

"I plan, you execute… Sound good?"

"Not really." He plucked the foil packet from her hand and sat up with his back against the cement wall. He got busy, ripping a corner of the packet and extracting the condom. "We do this together or not at all."

"I love a man with principles," Nina said, teasing, and inched closer to loosen his hair tie. She ran her fingers playfully through his thick waves. A lock of hair tumbled over his forehead. She leaned in and took his earlobe between her teeth and tugged.

He drew her onto his lap. "Come to me, baby."

She loved how solid he felt in her arms, loved the steady drumming of his heart. Her own pulse was erratic, her heart skipping wildly. The kiss she gave him was just as wild. He tilted her backward to some degree and fit himself inside her. Nina went rigid at first. Then warmth spread through her, and she relaxed in his arms. She dug her fingers in his hair, breathed him in, tasted him and moved with him. And then they took off, driving faster, harder, until they reached a climax that left her shattered. Nina collapsed against him, certain that he would collect her scattered pieces and keep her safe.

*Journal Entry*

*The sense of urgency is gone when we finally stumble into the suite and strip away our fussy dinner clothes once and for all. I fall into bed; the silky sheets feel delicious. Julian locks the door and joins me, kneeling at the foot of the bed. He takes hold of my hips and drags me to him. Aching with anticipation, I grab a pillow, anything to anchor me. "Hold on to me," he says in a low voice that makes me shudder. I reach for him and dig my fingers into his shoulders. When our eyes meet, the mix of turmoil and tenderness in his scares me. I know this thing with Julian is going to undo me. It may well break me. I know it and want it anyway.*

# Eleven

Julian assisted Nina down the stone steps leading to the sidewalk and for a while they stood still, fingers linked, in the flow of pedestrian traffic. He grinned down at her. He could not stop grinning. All day it was as if he were walking on clouds.

"Just us?" she said. "No driver or entourage?"

"Just us."

"Are you sure you can get away with this?"

"I can get away with a whole lot. Haven't you noticed?"

The bell tolled the hour, and all the memories of the night before came tumbling back, every wicked thing they'd done in the tower. By the look on Nina's face, he was sure her thoughts mirrored his.

"Let's go," he said. "The sooner we're done with dinner, the sooner we can revisit the tower. But if you need an entourage, I can get Pete to drive us."

"No, thanks," she said. "To be honest, I find Pete strange. Don't you?"

"He's all right. Only trying to get a day's work in."

Julian slipped an arm around her waist and got them moving in the direction of the restaurant.

"No..." She leaned into him. "My instincts aren't wrong. You should be careful around him."

He didn't question her instincts, but everyone in his orbit was bound to act strange at some point. It was only one of the many downsides of fame. And one complaint to management could get the man fired.

"I should be careful around *you*," he said. "You look dangerously good tonight."

If he couldn't address her concerns, the best he could do was lighten the mood. His strategy worked. She broke away. The straps of her short cotton sundress fell off her shoulders. "Then maybe you should keep your distance."

That was the one thing Julian did not have the strength to do. He chased after her and pinned her to him. "I'll keep my eye on Pete," he said. "I promise."

"Thanks," she said. "Now feed me."

The hotel concierge had recommended Ocra, a trendy Jamaican restaurant on Tenth Street well within walking distance from Sand Castle. There was no stuffy maître d' to contend with, only a friendly hostess who tripped on her words when Julian and Nina entered. The manager, a jovial man named Cyril, took over her duties. Grinning from ear to ear, he led them to a private table in the back of the restaurant. They were stopped along the way by patrons leaping out of their chairs, requesting selfies or just a hug. Julian obliged them, doling out hugs and posing for photos without once letting go of Nina's hand.

"Sorry about that," Cyril said when they finally reached their table. "You're Jamaica's favorite son."

Julian stood aside so Nina could slide into the booth. "I think Usain Bolt has that honor."

"He's never eaten here, and tonight you honor us." He handed Nina a menu with a little bow. "Welcome to Ocra, miss."

She smiled, looking amused at all the fuss. "Thank you."

Cyril left them to study the menu. Julian slid to her side of the booth.

The white flared skirt barely reached her midthigh. He reached down and nudged it higher.

"Stop it," she said, her eyes on the menu. "You'll have us thrown out for indecency."

"Impossible." Julian lowered his head and tugged at her ear with his teeth. "I'm the island's favorite son."

"Second only to Usain Bolt."

"I'll take it," Julian said. "What looks good?"

"Everything! I'd like to try this."

She pointed to a cocktail on the beverage menu: the Smoke Show. It was a mix of mescal, agave and smoked bell pepper.

"Really? I would have pegged you for a cranberry vodka girl."

"I told you, caution is out the window."

"I love the sound of that."

They kissed. It started light and deepened quickly. He pulled away, frustrated and out of breath. They were one click away from starring in another viral video.

She reached for her water glass and took a gulp. He did the same.

Julian had missed her, having spent the day at Frank's house, which was now, for all intents and purposes, ground zero. Frank's contacts in the business surpassed Julian's. By the end of the day, they were in talks with an independent production company, fleshing out a distribution deal. They'd discussed casting at length, which brought him to a pressing topic he wanted to discuss with Nina. He would have brought it up the minute he'd gotten back to Sand Castle, only he'd found Nina stretched out on the floor in cutoff denim shorts and a halter top. The printed manuscript was strewn out on the antique rug with notes in the margin.

"Don't touch anything," she said. "I gave it a closer read. I need to get into the characters' heads."

He walked over to her, sidestepping the pages like so many land mines. She rolled onto her back, a satisfied look on her face.

"I'd like to get in those shorts," he said, kneeling low to rub her flat belly.

"Not until you feed me," she said. "I've been snacking on granola bars all day."

"Want to get out of here?"

"Sure," she said. "But I've run out of fancy dresses. I only packed two, the one I drowned in and the one you made a mess of last night."

There was a blotch of blue ink on her cheek. He rubbed it away with the pad of his thumb. "No fancy dress. No problem."

By the time her cocktail was served, Julian had still not mustered the courage to share his news. He didn't want anything to sour their evening.

"I'd like to try the jerk chicken, the jerk corn and maybe a side of peas and rice," she said. "How about you?"

"The oxtail," he said without consulting the menu. No self-respecting Jamaican joint would lack an oxtail dish.

"But you're vegetarian!" she protested.

"Mostly vegetarian," he said. "After the night I had, I could eat anything."

She shut the menu and sent it sliding across the wood-plank table. "Really? My night was pretty tame."

She was joking, he knew it, but his pride took a blow. "You're younger than me by a few years, with way more stamina."

"No," she said with a crooked smile. "Your stamina is second only to Usain Bolt."

"What do you know about Bolt's stamina?"

"Only what I've seen on TV."

The manager returned to take their orders and to present them with an assortment of appetizers—a sample of the house's *likkle* plates. But as soon as he was gone, Nina pressed a kiss on Julian's cheek and whispered, "You're second to no one." Julian could not be prouder if he won a gold medal.

"I have to tell you something," he said.

"Yes?" she said, eyeing the platter of plantain bites, ackee rolls and salt-fish fritters. He thought he'd lost her, but after she bit into a fritter, moaned, rolled her eyes and broke into a happy dance, she reminded him that he had something to tell her.

"We had a discussion about casting today, Frank and I."

"You're still playing Luke, right?"

"Definitely."

The role in question was the lead: heiress Amanda King. Years ago, he'd offered it to Bettina. When he mentioned it to Frank, he took to the idea and wouldn't let it go. This left Julian the unenviable task of pushing back without coming off as a colossal jerk. "She won't work with me."

"Is it that bad between you two?"

It wasn't that bad, but it wasn't good. "Picture working with any one of your ex-wives?"

Frank had ignored his question and enlisted an impartial arbitrator. He got Karen Butler of B Plus Casting on the phone.

Karen was known in the industry for an open approach to casting actors in parts. As an African American actor whose prospects had dried up soon after she hit forty, Karen had started her agency with an aim to keeping underrepresented actors employed. Julian felt sure she wouldn't advocate for Bettina, but she did.

"I haven't read the script, so I can't say that she's right for the part you have in mind," Karen said. "But working together on a meaningful project would go a long way to shore up goodwill. You need that right now."

"She's not interested in helping me," Julian said.

Karen had a different take. "She'd be helping herself. I know on good authority that she doesn't have many offers in the pipeline. The controversy damaged both of you—no offense."

"None taken."

Julian had agreed to offer her the part. A phone call wasn't going to do it. Tomorrow he was flying out to Georgia, where Bettina was filming her television series, to offer her the part in person. First, he wanted to know how Nina felt about it.

"Frank thinks Bettina Ford would be right for the part of Amanda."

"Ah." She fell back against the cushion of the leather banquette. "What about you? What do you think?"

"I think she'd do a good job," Julian said. "I've always thought so. We've discussed it in the past. Even though I don't think she'll want the job, I should at least run it by her."

"What if she says yes?"

Her interest in the food had waned, which was unfortunate, because he knew she was hungry. He should have waited to tell her. Now he had no choice but to go all in. "You know about Betty and me, right? How things ended?"

It might have been his imagination, but Nina flinched when he mentioned Bettina by her nickname.

"I know what I read. I'd rather hear it from you."

As with everything, it started with a social media post. In this case, it was a tweet. He pulled it up and handed Nina the phone. She read it, grimaced and returned his phone.

Julian had it memorized. *When your so-called action-hero boyfriend is too limp to stand up for you, it's time to move on. #Bye.*

"Betty deleted it a half hour later, but the harm was done. Our breakup was announced on the news. Rather than overwork our publicists, we just went for it. We were done."

"Did you stand up for her?" she asked.

"I had it out with the director. I even threatened to bail on promotion." His answer seemed to ease Nina's concerns, but Julian didn't want to leave her with any misconceptions. "I stood up for her because she was my girlfriend, not because I cared about the big-picture implications of cutting her role out of the film. That came later."

"I get that you're not the most enlightened of your species, Julian. But you're not an ogre, either. You can stop beating yourself up already."

Julian wanted to believe her, but somehow she only saw the good in him. Her judgment had to be skewed.

"It's time you distinguish yourself from the balloon animal they've made you into."

She wasn't wrong. At some level, he believed every word printed about him. He let it define him, and to some degree he let it hold him back. It had almost stopped him from pursuing Nina, whom he considered a serious artist. It was unlikely one prickly tweet would damage her career.

"Today I focused on your character," Nina said, switching topics. "His lines have to be memorable."

"Going forward, should I sleep with all my screenwriters?" he wondered aloud. "No one's given a damn until this point."

"You could try," she said, her tone serious. "Why not?"

"I was being cheeky. You know that, right?"

"I wasn't."

He picked up a fritter and bit into it. He loved that she didn't cringe at his cringe-worthy jokes.

"If you want me to work extra hard, you'll have to motivate me," she said. "We have four nights left."

He nearly choked on the fritter. "Only four?"

She gave him a funny look. "Vacation is over."

"I thought you'd stay. Since you're working with us and everything."

"I can write from anywhere," she said with a shrug. "Might as well do it from my desk at home."

The strap of her dress finally fell over her narrow shoulder, but he was too distracted to care. Her dismissive tone unnerved him. "If that's true, you can stay and write here."

"No." She was firm. "I need my laptop and its stand, my wrist brace, special noise-canceling headphones, leggings and cozy slippers."

The waiter cleared the table and served their main dishes while Julian fumed. He was not going to let a pair of cozy slippers get between him and Nina. "Couldn't we have all of that shipped from Amazon?"

"No!" she objected. "I need *my* things. And I need clothes. These are my vacation clothes. There's not much to them."

"I like your vacation clothes," he said, tugging at the strap of her sundress.

She slapped his hand away. "We have to eat our food before it gets cold or Cyril will be insulted."

"I can't have that."

Julian picked up his utensils and attacked his oxtail without tasting it. He had no explanation for it, but the thought of her leaving filled him with dread. She probably had a full life to return to. He was asking for too much. Come to think of it, he hadn't asked for anything at all. Maybe he should try.

Julian laid down his fork and knife. "Stay with me. Don't you want to?"

She swallowed hard, although she hadn't been eating for a while. "It's not that simple."

"I can make it simple."

Having her stuff shipped was no big deal. If she

needed to fly to New York and take care of things, he could arrange that, too. Needless to say, she didn't have to worry about running a tab at Sand Castle. He'd take care of it. There were no logistical problems that money couldn't solve. He didn't want to put it so bluntly, but that was the truth.

Her grip tightened on her fork. "I don't want to discuss this anymore."

They finished their meal in near silence and walked back to the hotel. The usual group of tourists had gathered outside the hotel gates, cell phones in hand. Julian signaled one of the guards to assist them, but he took the lead, shielding Nina. She hooked a finger through a loop of his jeans and did not let go, following him to the lift. When the doors slid shut, she swiveled around and buried his face in his chest. Julian held her close. He finally tasted relief.

She slipped her arms around his waist. "Ask me again tomorrow. Okay?"

"Sorry. I don't think I can relive the trauma."

"Just do it, please."

"Why?" He smoothed her hair. "Do you need time to overthink it?"

"Something like that."

Julian did not her ask again. Instead, the next morning, he inquired about something less incendiary.

"The left one is larger than the right?"

She curled up to him. "Yup!"

"I'm left-handed, so that's perfect." To prove his point, he cupped her left breast with his left hand. It fit perfectly.

"You're left-handed?" she asked.

"I am. Is that a deal breaker?"

"Only for my right breast."

"Don't worry," he said. "I got it covered."

He bit down on her right nipple and sucked until he heard her moan. Every day should start like this, except it was already lunchtime. They'd slept in. Sunlight burst through the stained glass windows, fighting its way into their cocoon. And he was hungry.

She reached down and cupped him between the legs, startling him. "Are these a matching set?"

"Don't, Nina," he warned. "You'll wake up the Knight."

"Wait! What?" She pulled away from him and sat up on her knees. "Is that what you call it?"

"It suits him, don't you think? He's honorable and brave."

"Brave?" She laughed. "He bravely goes where no man—"

He pinched her chin between his thumb and index finger and pulled her in for a kiss. "Silly woman."

"Is he dependable?" she asked.

"Rain or shine, gets the job done."

"Maybe we shouldn't talk about him as if he's not in the room."

Julian agreed. "His ego is pretty fragile."

"Why? He's such a tall, proud soldier."

"A knight. Please don't mess with his title." He reached for the room service menu on the bedside table. "Breakfast?"

"Yes, please." She tossed aside the crumpled bedsheet and knelt between his legs. "I could eat."

He closed his eyes. His last coherent thought was that he must be the luckiest bastard in the world.

# Twelve

Nina was curled up in the wide bed, listening to the sounds of Julian in the shower, when her phone rang. It was on the nightstand next to Julian's two mobile phones and his array of chargers. Seeing their devices lumped together like that bothered her. It looked to her as if they were becoming a couple. Rattled, she reached for her phone and answered without first checking the caller ID. "Hello."

"Hey, Nina? It's me. Checking in again."

"Valerie?"

"Yes," she said. "I was in the neighborhood and decided to stop by your hotel."

"Excuse me?" Nina stammered.

"You're here, right? Staying at the Sand Castle."

"Yes."

"Well, I'm downstairs. In the courtyard. Are you free to chat?"

Nina sat up and drew the blanket over her bare legs. There was no question her cousin had seen the photos and read the blog posts. Her identity was no longer a mystery, and her social media accounts were clogged with mentions. No doubt Valerie wanted to check in on the state of her mental health. Was it out of character for Nina to hook up with a high-profile movie star? Absolutely. Was it any of her cousin's business? Absolutely not. But Nina hadn't grown up in a tight-knit nuclear family, and she was fuzzy on the rules. What was the best way to deal with an interfering but well-meaning cousin without coming off as rude?

Nina lowered the phone to her bare chest and took a few sharp breaths to calm down. It didn't work. Through clenched teeth, she said, "I'll be right down."

Ten minutes later, Nina came down the grand stairway in the same frilly dress she'd worn out to dinner the night before. Valerie Pierre, a lawyer, looked polished in a blue pantsuit. A curvy woman with deep brown skin, she wore her hair in a cropped Afro. She stood by the fountain, scrolling on her phone. Nina hadn't seen her since her mother's funeral. Valerie was the only relative on her father's side of the family who had bothered to show up. The others sent flowers, food and money. For that reason, she couldn't kick her to the curb—as much as she wanted to.

"Hey there," Nina said with an awkward wave.

"Nina!"

Valerie rushed over and pulled her into a hug. Her genuine warmth melted away Nina's icy irritation. They ended up at a table on the terrace with coffee and pastries.

"Don't worry," Valerie said, eyeing her from behind her large glasses. "I'll be out of your hair soon. I have to get back to work."

"There's no rush. It'll be great to catch up."

Valerie pursed her lips. "Yeah. I'm just going to jump right in."

Nina gave her a blank smile. "What do you mean?"

"Okay. So, last night, I was clicking around the web for reviews of *Thunder III*. Patrick wanted to stream it, but I'd heard some negative things."

Nina smirked at the mention of Valerie's husband. It was like Julian had said—women rarely owned up to liking the films. It was always a boyfriend or husband. Men did the same with dance or baking competition shows. It was always the girlfriend or wife who made them tune in every week.

She handed Nina her phone. "Then I stumble on this."

Nina pinched the screen to zoom in on the offensive content. A website had put together a slideshow of her and Julian's courtship in chronological order under the headline, *Love Him or Hate Him, JL Knight Heats Things Up in Miami*.

Photo #1: *JLK and Nina Taylor\* on a balcony at Sand Castle gaze into each other's eyes behind a veil of summer rain. #Meetcute?*

Photo #2: *JLK dives into a pool—fully dressed— to rescue his girl. #RescueMeJLK*

Photo #3: *JLK assists his lady friend into a waiting car, his hand dangerously close to her ass. #PDA*

Photo #4: *JLK kisses his woman under the stars. #TrueLoveKiss*

(*Nina Taylor is an author. Her memoir, *Backstage Diva*, debuted at number seventeen on the *NYT* bestseller list.)

The last photo was of her and Julian's first kiss. It was the one photo of the bunch that truly upset her. She would have liked to keep that moment private. The sneaky photographer had caught an intimate moment. That night she had suspected they were being watched, and now she had proof. It *had* to have been Pete. He was the only one lurking around that night.

"Those photos are misleading." Nina tried to rationalize the irrational. "He did rescue me and we went out a few times, but there's nothing to that kiss and—"

Valerie reached across the table and squeezed her hand. "I'm not here to pry. But this is a whole lot of drama and I'm concerned, that's all."

"We're working together." Nina regretted the words almost immediately. Had Julian expected her to keep it confidential?

Valerie made a face. "Working on what? Not another *Thunder* movie!"

"I'm not at liberty to say. And please don't tell anyone."

"Nina," Valerie said gravely, "that guy hooks up with every one of his costars. Don't you keep up with this stuff?"

Nina realized that her smart-girl image, her large-and-in-charge persona, was a liability. Valerie couldn't imagine her having a vacation fling or even having fun. Any outlandish behavior on her part, any bit of drama, had to be a cry for help.

"Scratch that," Valerie said. "Your sex life is none of my business. Just make sure any contract you sign is airtight. The last woman he worked with got cut from his movie. And they were engaged, too."

"They were *not* engaged." For whatever reason, Nina was eager to clarify this point.

"Wait," Valerie said, looking past Nina's shoulder. "Is that him?"

A quick glance in the direction that Valerie had hinted at confirmed that it was in fact Julian and he was making his way toward their table. As always, the sight of him thrilled her. He looked fresh in his usual T-shirt and jeans. Her gaze fell to the travel bag slung over his shoulder, and she recalled that he was flying to Atlanta to speak with Bettina. Nina took a sip of coffee to cure a sudden headache.

"Heading out to the airport," he said. "Thought I'd say goodbye."

"And I'd like to say hello." Valerie popped up and introduced herself. "Hi! I'm Valerie Pierre, Nina's cousin."

"Nice to meet you. I didn't know Nina had family in Miami."

He went on to ask her where she lived and what she did for a living. And for a while they chatted like old friends. Valerie was obviously starstruck. Her bright eyes, overly broad smile and unbridled laughter were dead giveaways. Nina was baffled. How quickly the ice had thawed! Considering Valerie's low opinion of Julian, this was an astonishing 180.

When the time came to say goodbye, Nina caught the hesitation in Julian's eyes. He made no attempt to hug or kiss her, no doubt dissuaded by her stiff body language. He waved, and she waved back. Once he was out of her sight, it was all Nina could do to keep from chasing after him.

She'd played this wrong, waffling in front of her cousin like that. Julian wasn't much older than her, but it was likely he'd matured past the need to play games. Except she was genuinely freaking out. Despite photo slideshows proving the contrary, she'd enjoyed their relative privacy. This hotel was their safe haven. She wasn't ready to answer questions about their relationship.

Valerie settled back in her seat. "So…that's Julian."

Nina nodded slowly. "That's Julian."

"I like him. He seems cool."

Nina was so relieved that she broke out in a cold sweat. It scared her how badly she wanted Valerie to like him, to differentiate the man in the crappy movie from the man she was sharing a bed with. At the same time, it saddened Nina that she needed outside validation.

"The rumors are true," Nina blurted. "Everything you've read about us is true. We're…" She searched for an elegant term and came up short. "We're hooking up."

"I hope so!" Valerie said. "Imagine coming all this way for an intervention and have nothing to intervene in. Do you know how much it costs to park on Ocean Drive?"

Nina wondered why an intervention was even required. "Is it so crazy what I'm doing?"

Valerie fixed her with her amber eyes. "Honestly? Yes. But just because it's crazy doesn't mean you shouldn't do it. Life is short. You'll need an exit strategy, though. Do you have one?"

Nina stared into her empty coffee cup. Sooner or later,

she and Julian would part ways and return to their respective worlds. That wasn't so much a strategy as the charted course of a doomed voyage.

# Thirteen

Julian stood watching Bettina tumble into bed with a much younger man—younger than him, anyway. The guy was shirtless, hairless and slim. Bettina wore a white towel around her torso. In a moment or so, it would fall away. But this being Hollywood, nothing was as it appeared. Bettina was playing the role of Jennifer Duncan, a prosecutor who, for whatever reason, was sleeping with a key witness in a high-profile case. The man who played her lover was Pierce Alexander, an acclaimed film actor gunning for an Emmy. Finally, they weren't on a Hollywood back lot, but a soundstage in Atlanta.

Bettina and Pierce kissed with abandon until the director yelled, "Cut!"

Bettina pulled herself up and darted a look his way, her face tight with frustration. She raised an index finger. *One sec.*

Julian shrugged. *Take your time.*

He missed being in a long-term relationship. He loved the shorthand couples shared, even when it was passive-aggressive as hell.

Bettina and her costar huddled with the director for a few minutes, then she hobbled over in fuzzy slippers. Her red hair was damp and brushed away from her face. Her eye makeup was artfully smudged, and her freckles were double the actual amount. This was her third season playing Jennifer Duncan, a civil servant who managed to live in great style on a state government salary.

"Thanks for meeting me here," she said. "Can't do lunch. We don't have Pierce for long, so we'll be working through the day."

Julian cocked his head, a nice way of saying. *Screw Pierce.* Seeing her on set with the actor had triggered a jolt of jealousy. But it wasn't fresh emotion, just something warmed up from the past, and he knew it.

"How about later? Come to the hotel. We'll have a drink at the bar."

Bettina searched his face with those clever green eyes. "A rendezvous at a hotel bar? That's not what exes do."

That wasn't what he was proposing. He simply didn't want to offer her a job while on the set of her current job. "I'm clear on that."

Julian's palms were sweating. He shoved his hands in his back pockets and thrust out his chest. Bettina caught the gesture and laughed. "You're nervous! Could you come out with it? I don't have all day."

He came out with it. "Betty, where do you stand on us working together again?"

"You and me?"

"Yes."

"Christ, no!" She recoiled from him. "Haven't we been through enough?"

The director called out her name and held up five fingers. "Got it!" she fired back and turned to Julian. "Just curious. What project did you have in mind?"

*"Midnight Sun."*

She laughed again, her bare shoulders bobbing. More freckles had been painted there, too. "Your *pet* project?"

He waited for the barb to lose its sting. They were regressing. It was starting to feel like old times. Except this tense exchange wasn't about her choice of restaurant or his pile of clothes on the bathroom floor. This concerned their careers and everything they'd worked so hard to achieve. Bettina would be phenomenal in the role of Amanda King. He'd written the role with her in mind. But this project was supposed to mark a fresh start. How could they move forward if they were forever in each other's way?

"Sorry," she said. "That came out wrong."

The apology threw Julian off the path he was heading down. He stared at her without understanding. Bettina *never* apologized; at best she shared the blame.

"Don't look so shocked. I'm working on myself."

For the year that they'd been apart, Julian had been working on himself, too. But he'd been so close to walking out on Bettina just now, which was his MO. The theatrical exit was a signature move. Also, he had a tendency to be pushy. He could no longer deny that he'd been pushy with Nina. He'd pushed her into accepting to work on the script and again, last night, he'd pushed her to agree to stay. It had to stop. His bullishness stemmed from fear of losing her. He was sure they were at the start of something significant, but they needed time.

The director shouted, "Actors on set!"

Bettina snapped to attention. "You've got to go, Julian. The next scene is a closed set."

He played his last card. "I don't know if this makes a difference, but Francisco Cortes is directing."

Bettina was walking away backward and came close to knocking over a piece of lighting equipment. She stopped short. "For real?"

"I wouldn't make it up."

"Quiet on set!" the director bellowed.

Bettina waved goodbye and went back to work. A makeup artist approached her and began dabbing her forehead with a sponge. Julian exited the brick building at end of an alley lined with similarly bland buildings. The sky was the color of ash, and rain made the sidewalk slick. The driver sprang out of the car with an umbrella, but Julian was quick to slide into the back seat unassisted.

"To the W, Mr. Knight?"

"No. The airport."

Just as the car pulled away from the curb, he caught sight of Bettina, yanking on a robe as she stepped out of the building. Julian asked the driver to wait and rolled down the window. "What is it?"

She shielded her eyes from the sting of rain. "Send me the script. I can't promise anything, but I'll read it."

"I can't ask for more," Julian said. "Now get back inside. Pierce is waiting."

She gave him the finger. He blew her a kiss.

Nina spent the rest of the day working on the script. In the evening, she took her journal to the garden. She was greeted by the smell of freshly cut grass and nothing else. She had expected to find Grace enjoying a glass of wine, but the garden was empty. She paid respects to the goddess Aphrodite, plopped down in a rattan chair and flipped open her journal, picking up where she'd left off.

*"You look lonely in there."*

*"You mean peaceful. I'm at peace in here."*

*"Well...we can't have that."*

*Julian climbs into the tub. Water splashes everywhere, creating puddles on the marble floor. I give him my expert Goldilocks assessment. "This tub is too small!"*

*"Feels just right to me."*

*Our wet hands grab for each other, and his feels just right in mine. I fit him inside me. His moan is just a rumble in his chest. He nudges a lock of damp hair away from my ear and murmurs, "I could drown in you."*

*I'm drowning already. He cradles me, lifts me, but I refuse to be rescued—not this time, not again.*

Nina tucked the pen between the pages. The memory overwhelmed her. Thoughts of Julian had tugged at her all day. She hated the way they'd left things—without even a hug goodbye. He hadn't called all day; it was quiet on all fronts. She would have welcomed anything—a briefly worded text or simply a thumbs-up emoji. Plus, the larger question still loomed. Was she staying or leaving or what? He hadn't asked. After spending the day with Bettina, would he have a change of heart?

"Good evening, Ms. Taylor."

Grace arrived, looking more somber than a woman swinging an ice bucket fitted with a glistening bottle of wine had any right to be.

"Your Grace," Nina said with a little bow. "What do you have for us this evening?"

"A fine prosecco."

"Perfect."

Grace set down the bucket and two stemless champagne flutes. Nina wondered if she was always prepared for company or if she was expecting someone in particular. Either way, she accepted a glass of the sparkling wine.

Grace took her glass to her lips, sipped from it and let out a soft sigh. *"Qué rico."*

It truly was a rich experience: the warm evening, the wine, the fragrant garden, the mansion gleaming like polished ivory against the darkening sky. "Can you believe this house once belonged to a single family?" Nina said.

"I can," Grace said. "It belongs to my family now."

Nina jerked forward, and drops of prosecco flew onto her lap. "You own this hotel?"

"My father does. I run the day-to-day operations."

No wonder Grace carried herself like the grande dame of the château! It all made sense. But it didn't explain Grace's chronic dissatisfaction. Wealth, position and beauty—she'd inherited the trifecta. What exactly was her problem?

Voices rose in the courtyard, a chorus of "Welcome back, Mr. Knight!"

The hotel staff loved Julian. He was always polite and greeted everyone by name. Nina bolted her rear end to her chair. She would not dart out of the garden and tackle him. For one thing, she would not give Grace the satisfaction.

In the end, it was Grace that offered her an out. "Any dinner plans tonight? It's later than you may think. Shouldn't you be getting ready?"

"You're right." Nina stood up. "I should get going."

"Enjoy dinner, Ms. Taylor."

"Thank you. Enjoy your night, Grace."


Julian was on the grand staircase, scaling the stairs by two. Nina had to sprint to catch up to him. When he left with an overnight bag, she worried that she might have to spend a night without him, which would be a first since arriving in Miami. The idea had terrified her. "Hey!" she called out. "You're back!"

He didn't hide his delight in seeing her, drawing her to him for a kiss. Nina stiffened only because she was aware of Pete entering the courtyard. He had likely picked Julian up from the airport. He went over to the front desk and just lingered there. But even Pete couldn't distract her for too long. She shook off her worries and relaxed into Julian's kiss. Let the world see. Let them post about it. And when their relationship came to its inevitable end, let them tweet up a storm. This time together in Miami could be all they'd ever have, and she didn't want to ruin it with doubts and fears. She was going to live it fully.

"I need a shower before dinner," he said. "Want to come up with me to Paradise?"

"You mean Oasis."

"I said what I said. It's paradise with you."

"Fine!" Nina cried, as if she weren't elated beyond words. "I'll grab a few things."

Arm in arm, they made their way up the winding stairs. "Enjoyed your day?" he asked.

"It was productive."

In truth, her day hadn't been as productive as Nina would have liked. She'd wasted a good chunk of time scrolling through photos of JL and Bettina in happier times. They made a handsome couple; there was no denying it. His dark good looks contrasted with her pale beauty. On the red carpet, they flashed matching smiles. With each swipe, jealousy had churned in her chest.

"How was your trip? Did she say yes?"

"She didn't say no."

They'd reached her door. "If she says yes, I'll make sure she has killer lines."

She had little doubt Bettina would accept the role of Amanda King—it was that good.

He wrapped his arms around her and planted a kiss in the curve of her neck. "How are you so lovely and generous?"

Nina unlocked the door and switched on the lights. Julian abandoned her for her bed, stretching out with a sigh of contentment. Nina watched him from the foot of the bed. He likely sensed her looming over him. "Did you forget the plan? Go on. Grab what you need."

"Yeah. Right." She went into the bathroom and blindly stuffed a few toiletries into a case.

"You okay?" Julian called out from the bedroom.

"I'm fine!"

She wasn't, of course, and couldn't explain why. A minute ago, she was joy personified. She returned to the bedroom and grabbed her travel tote bag from the armoire.

"Are you sure about that?" Julian asked. He was propped up on one elbow, watching her. "Did I say something wrong?"

"Yeah!" she said, awakening to the truth. "I'm not lovely or generous."

"You're not?"

"No! I'm jealous."

He sat up, all of a sudden alert, bright-eyed, engaged. "Tell me more."

"I spent the day looking at—" She bit down on her lower lip, thinking it might be best to keep the crazy details to herself. "I was worried that you two—" Was there any way to talk about this without sounding like a complete basket case?

"You were worried that Bettina and I would take one look at each other and fall back in love?"

"Something like that."

He reached out to her, wrapped his hand around her wrist and tugged her close. She stood between his parted knees. "It was nothing like that. I promise you. We spoke for all of ten minutes. Then I left and headed straight back to the airport. I spent the day at the lounge, waiting for clearance to fly. I didn't want to waste any of the few nights we have left."

Nina's heart was hammering in her chest. "Ask me again."

A spark of hope brightened his expression. "Have you had enough time to think it through? I don't want to rush you."

Nina took his face in her hands and ran her fingers

along the angles. Stubble pricked her fingertips. "Just ask me."

He took her wrist to his lips. "Stay. Please."

He wasn't asking. He was pleading. Her response was a plea as well. She circled her arms around his neck and slid onto his lap. "Hold me. Don't let me go."

# Fourteen

Nina had long forgotten that disastrous commercial flight to Miami, and the delays and inconveniences that came standard with flying coach, when she boarded the private jet chartered to take her home. And now, at cruising altitude, sitting across from a handsome movie star, sipping espresso from a porcelain cup, a cashmere throw on her lap and no packets of peanuts or granola bars anywhere in sight, Nina wondered if she'd won some cosmic lottery. It was a good thing that clawing anxiety kept things in perspective. *Too good to be true is no good at all*, her mother used to say.

They were leaving Miami to spend the night at her tiny New York apartment. When Julian had offered to fly her home and back, she'd said yes before she had a chance to think it through. Her place lacked the comforts he was accustomed to—specifically, room service, fluffy white towels and housekeeping. Her apartment was a mess. Her plants had likely withered in her absence, and there was a high chance that leftover takeout was rotting in her fridge.

There was no time to worry about it during the drive into the city. She and Julian read lines in the back seat of the town car as the driver zipped through tunnels only to slow to a crawl as traffic picked up.

"'Day. Pool. Amanda floats on her back,'" Julian said, reading from his copy of the script. "'The man who spent the night approaches, fully dressed, and tells her that he's leaving. Amanda swims to the pool's edge.

"'Man says, "This was fun, babe. Let's do this again soon."

"'Amanda says, "Sure. You have my number.""'

Nina shook her head. "No…"

"You don't like it?"

"I hate it." Not every one of Amanda's lines had to be a zinger, but they couldn't fall flat, either. She jotted a few notes before reading aloud to him.

"'Man says, "Gotta go, babe. Let's do this again soon." Amanda, flirting, splashes him with water, and says, "But not too soon. Okay?""'

Nina checked Julian's reaction. He stared down at the words on the page, his jaw tight. "It's a small change that does two things," she said. "This is the opening scene, and it ought to show Amanda's cocky playfulness. Plus, it wraps up this story. The audience won't expect to see this guy again."

"Brilliant," Julian murmured. "You're such a natural, Nina."

Nina thought of all the hours she'd spent at the breakfast table, spooning cereal into her mouth and reading her mother's scripts. It was paying off.

"I should have asked for more money."

"Too late. The contract is signed," he said. "Come here and I'll make up the difference."

She released her seat belt and would have climbed onto his lap if the driver hadn't pulled up to her building.

Julian was looking out the window, assessing her tidy redbrick building on Manhattan's Lower East Side. Nina didn't wait for the driver. She pushed open the door and climbed out. The sounds of the city swirled around her. No loud, drunken tourists or reggaeton blasting from convertibles here—only the sounds of the punishing pursuit of ambition. However temporary, it was good to be home.

Nina froze at the sight of a pink upholstered couch sitting on the curb. She recognized it instantly, having spent many evenings curled up on it, drinking wine and binge-watching nineties-era sitcoms. It belonged to her friend and neighbor, decor fanatic Laetitia. What was it doing on the curb? If her friend had grown tired of it, Nina would have gladly taken it off her hands.

As Julian tipped the driver, Nina pulled out her phone, snapped a photo of the couch and sent it to Laetitia. Within seconds, her friend called, shouting, "What in the world?"

"You tell me."

"Freaking Ted! He's moving out and being a colossal jerk about it."

Ted was moving out? Hell yeah! He'd always been a colossal jerk. It had taken Laetitia this long to figure it out. But still, what was the couch doing on the curb? "Is he tossing out your stuff?"

"He bought it for me as a birthday gift," Laetitia whispered. She was at work and probably hiding in a bathroom stall for some privacy. "He knows how much I love it."

A woman walking a dog tore off her earbuds and lunged toward the couch. Before she could thank her lucky stars, Nina chased her away. "Back away from the couch, lady!" Both the woman and her cocker spaniel growled at Nina and pranced off.

On the phone Laetitia was freaking out. "Don't let anyone take my Jonathan Adler!"

"Okay, Laeti, but I can't watch over it all day."

In her frustration, Nina turned to Julian. He stood leaning against the town car, arms folded, watching her with eyes sparkling with amusement. Nina lowered the phone and got him up to speed. "It's a Jonathan Adler, and it's beautiful."

He laughed and looked up at the hazy sky. "I appreciate the irony of my having to point this out, but this is a classic example of first-world problems."

"Julian! We don't have time for your musings."

"What do you want to do? Take it to your apartment?" He walked over to the couch, grabbed an armrest and lifted it with one hand. "It's not too heavy. I could use some help, though."

Nina swooned. Her very own action hero! Calm and composed and proposing solutions that actually made sense.

The driver offered his assistance. "I used to be a mover back in the day."

"Good," Julian said. "I'll make it worth your while."

Nina raised the phone to her ear. "Don't worry, Laeti. We have a plan."

"Who's the man with the voice like honey?" Laetitia asked.

"That's not important. We'll take it up to my place and—"

"No! Take it straight to mine! Ted is still there. I'll call him and straighten this out."

Nina was grateful. Her apartment would be cramped enough with Julian in it. She didn't need a large pink couch clogging up the foyer. Only this meant she'd have to confront the rabid ex-boyfriend. Anything for a friend, right? She would do it out of the kindness of her heart. "Hey, Laeti? You owe me big-time."

"Anything. I'll do your laundry if you want me to."

"I'm thinking dinner and drinks when I get back."

"Get back from where? You just got back."

"Can't get into it now! I'll fill you in later."

Nina ended the call and addressed her troops. "Okay, guys. We're taking it up to the third floor, apartment 3C. I'll hold the service elevator."

"Nice building," Julian observed as he carried his end of the couch through the lobby.

Holding the elevator as promised, Nina tried to see the space through the eyes of a millionaire movie star. It was well lit and clean. The frosted glass and gold accents did very little to elevate the plain design. "I'm sure you've lived in much nicer places."

"I have." He looked at her for a bit as if gauging if he should say more. Those quiet eyes always got to her. "But I've also lived in my car, so make what you want out of that."

Nina clutched the pair of bolster pillows to her chest. Why was she still struggling to see Julian as an ordinary person? She kept tripping over the same low wire. He was not an action hero or a movie star. He was just a guy who didn't hesitate to help lift a friend's couch off the curb.

He and the driver tried out different ways to fit the couch into the elevator until they got it right. On the ride up, he asked if Laetitia was a good friend of hers.

"Good enough," she said. "We binged an entire season of *Riverside Rescue* on this." Nina patted the couch standing upright between them. "That makes it worth saving, don't you think?"

Julian looked doubtful. "That's one opinion."

They reached the third floor. After some maneuvering, he and the driver moved the couch into the hall. She led them to Laetitia's door then swiveled around to give Julian a pointed look. "There's probably going to be some drama. I'll handle it."

"Whatever you say."

He backed away and leaned against the wall. Nina knocked on the apartment door. It wasn't locked and swung open. Ted looked up from a pile of boxes stacked like a pyramid where the couch should have been.

"Laetitia called," he said flatly. "Sorry for your wasted effort, but you're not bringing that thing in here. It's my couch. I bought it. I tossed it out. There's no law against it."

Judge Judy would have laughed that argument out of small claims court. "It was a gift, Ted."

"Mind your own business," Ted said. "And shut the door on your way out."

Nina was prepared for a little bit of back-and-forth,

but not this stonewalling. At a loss, she turned to Julian. She hated to be the girl who got her boyfriend to fight her battles, but Julian wasn't her boyfriend, so it didn't count. He responded to her silent plea with a wink. "Guess we'll do it my way."

She nodded and went to stand next to the driver, who, to his credit, had not lost his professional composure. Julian didn't move. He stayed as he was, leaning against the wall, and called out to Ted, "How do you want to do this?"

Gone were the accent and any gentlemanly manners. He'd transformed into his on-screen persona. Nina hated to admit it, but it was hot.

"Hey, Nina!" Ted said, waving a duct tape dispenser. "Where'd you get this impersonator? Vegas?"

Julian pushed off the wall and crowded the doorway. "I'm bringing in this couch. It would be a mistake to try to stop me. And if it lands on the curb again, I'll know. We won't be far." He turned to Nina. "Where's your apartment?"

"Ted knows," Nina said. "I'm down the hall. Apartment 3D."

Julian slipped out of character, a mischievous grin spreading across his face. "Three D? Really? Will we need special glasses?"

The man was a child! "Ha-ha! Three D! So funny! Could you wrap this up, please?"

He turned to Ted and resumed his admonishment. "Look. If I have to carry this couch, or anything else, back up here, you and I will have a problem."

Ted's reaction was staggered. He pinned a blank stare on Julian, puffed out his chest, rolled his hands into fists and stretched to his full height. It was comical to watch.

Julian could snap the stockbroker in two, but Nina knew he wouldn't.

"Are we going to have a problem, Ted?" Julian asked.

Ted deflated. "To hell with it. I don't care."

"Good man."

After Laetitia's couch was back in its place and the driver well compensated, Nina welcomed Julian to her apartment. She liked her place. It was small, a studio, but it didn't lack character. The wood parquet floors were beautiful. The living area was bright thanks to tall windows with immediate views of the tops of oak trees and a row of redbrick buildings farther down the street. Julian walked around in circles, commenting on framed photographs and book collections. Nina did not need 3D glasses to see him in all his complexity. He was a beautiful man, but he was more than that. He was smart, funny, generous, insightful and fair. He was tender, gentle, understanding… She saw him, and he *was* beautiful.

"Goldie, what are you overthinking now?"

He came to stand before her, hands low on his hips. Apparently, he didn't need special glasses to see her, either.

"I'm *thinking* this feels just right."

Julian wrapped her in his arms. It was everything and it was not enough. Nina needed to feel his skin against hers. She stepped back, unbuckled her jeans and shimmied to better push the stiff denim over her hips.

"What are you doing?" he asked.

"We're home," she said. "Time to slip into something more comfortable."

* * *

*Journal Entry*
    *"May I taste?"*
    *I nod, because the words won't come. He presses*
*me against the door and hunches low. I readily*
*hook a knee over his shoulder, but when his tongue*
*meets my tender skin, I'm not prepared for the*
*rush... I have to tug at his hair to keep from cry-*
*ing out.*
    *We haven't made it to the bed.*

# Fifteen

Cozy in her bed, limbs intertwined, Julian and Nina got back to work. Nina seemed giddy to be reunited with her laptop. She had hugged it to her chest and spun around like Maria in the opening credits of *The Sound of Music*. And now she leaned on his shoulder as they scrolled through actor profiles, looking to round out the cast. Julian was partial to a French actor, Vincent Gabriel, winner of a César and a BAFTA, to play the role of Luke's accomplice. If he were honest, Vincent would probably shine in the role of Luke—if he weren't hogging it for himself. Nina was a foreign film buff, and she melted at the mention of Vincent's name.

Julian pulled away from her. "What was that?"

"What was what?"

"You sighed."

"You're imagining things."

"Do you sigh at the mention of my name?" he asked.

"I've cried out your name at three in the morning," Nina said. "What more do you want?"

"More!"

She tossed her copy of the script to the floor. Its pages were bloodied with red ink. "Sorry. I don't have much more to give."

"Not sure I believe that, Goldie. I'll have to double my efforts tonight."

He reached for his phone to check the time. It was 10:35 p.m. and he had two missed calls—from a studio executive in California.

Eleven p.m. Julian was still on the phone, arguing with the executive. The production company was backing out from its agreement to fund *Midnight Sun*.

"You hired an unknown to revise the script and Francisco Cortes to direct. There's a stable of hotshot directors to choose from, and you went with Cortes."

"Frank has a vision—"

"I'm sure he does. He's not the right person to direct this film."

Julian was pacing a hole into Nina's wood floors. "I won't drop him."

"We're not asking you to. We're pulling funding from the film, and we wish you luck."

"You're making a mistake."

"Sorry, Knight. It's done."

Straightaway, Julian got Frank on the phone. Frank answered on the hundredth ring, his voice raspy. "At this hour it better be important."

"Spring Pictures dropped us."

"For what reason?"

Julian hesitated. "It doesn't matter."

"How much were they in for?"

"Half the budget."

Frank fell quiet, and Julian did, too. They were screwed, and they both knew it. Funding from an established production house would lend the film clout. What the hell were they going to do now?

Frank had the answer. "I'll put up the money."

"Don't do this."

"I've always wanted to produce. If we stick to our budget, we can manage. And I can bring in some very rich people who've been dying to get into the movie business."

Julian went weak with relief and leaned against Nina's breakfast bar. She was folding clothes into her suitcase, pretending not to eavesdrop. He hoped she hadn't overheard the producer taking him to task for hiring her. It was the one decision he would not overturn. He needed her. They worked well together. More than that, she made work fun and challenging. He did not need Hollywood's seal of approval on this.

"I have one condition."

Julian ran a hand through his hair. "You and your bloody conditions, Frank."

"I come aboard as a coproducer and you take the reins."

"I don't follow."

"This is your movie to direct. You know it."

"Like hell I do."

"Trust me, Julian," Frank said. "I know this business. It runs on stories. This is *your* comeback story, not mine. Julian Knight writes and directs his first feature film. How does that sound?"

It sounded so good, Julian's chest ached, but assuming the role of director scared him to death. The best directors he'd worked with were creative geniuses. That wasn't him.

"I know you can do it," Frank said. "And I know you *want* to do it. Take a chance. What do you have to lose?"

"Your money."

"There's more to life than money."

This paternal side to Francisco Cortes was endearing. "Do you have kids, Frank?"

"More than a few." He laughed. "Can you tell?"

Julian made up his mind. He'd do it under one condition. "I'm not acting in a film I'm directing. We'd have to find someone to play the part of Luke."

He had to draw the line somewhere. As the writer, director and producer, all the trappings of a vanity project were present and accounted for. Besides, he wouldn't have the time. He had two monumental tasks ahead: one, to deliver a film on time and on budget, and two, to coax subtle and nuanced performances from the cast. The second goal was arguably the most important. His acting skills were limited, and this film was so different from anything he'd ever been involved in. He'd never had an acting job that didn't involve a gun as a prop.

"Agreed," Frank said. "But that's a question for another day. I'm going back to sleep."

"Did I wake you, Dad?"

"I'll tell you what I tell my kids, Julian. Unless you're calling from jail, don't call me after 10:00 p.m."

"Gotcha."

Julian slid his phone across the countertop and pressed his forehead against the cool granite. "Nina," he groaned. "I need your loving."

"I've got something better." She walked into the kitchen, pulled a bottle out of the freezer and grabbed a couple glasses from the cupboard. "What was all that about?"

"The studio dropped us. Frank is producing. I'm directing and dropping the role of Luke." He looked down at the glass she put before him. "I'm going to need more vodka than this."

She splashed more Grey Goose in his glass. "I don't know. Sounds perfect to me. Everything is shaking into place."

*This woman*... In an oversize concert T-shirt and fuzzy slippers, hair in a topknot, she was at ease in her home. That overall glow was the result of his handiwork, and he was proud of it. The T-shirt, though, was a relic from the past. He'd asked if she was a fan of Bruce Springsteen. Although she was a fan, she confessed that the T-shirt belonged to an ex.

"Since everyone seems to be expanding their roles, maybe I should, too."

"Would you like to try acting? We could find you a role."

"No, Julian," she said. "I'm not a performer. I'm a storyteller."

She spoke with the confidence of a lifetime of soul searching, pen to paper, first filling countless pretty diaries with locks, then spiral-bound notebooks and now leather-bound journals. Julian admired this about her above all.

"You hired me to patch up the dialogue, but I could do more with the material if you trust me."

"Do what you want with it. I trust you more than myself." He had rushed to reassure her, only now he was curious as to what she had in mind. "What are your thoughts?"

"The Amanda story arc needs an overhaul."

"Overhaul?" He'd expected a tweak here and there, not an overhaul. "Are you sure?"

"She's either rebelling against her father, competing with her brother or reacting to Luke. She needs an arc independent of the men in her life."

"How about you write a monologue to address this?"

She rolled her eyes at him. "You'd have her stand on a mountain and preach the gospel of feminism?"

"I see your point." Amanda was the lead, and he wanted her role to be as strong as possible. He wouldn't want to be accused of failing another female character. On the other hand, there was a risk that pulling on one thread could unravel the whole story. "You think it's possible to undertake a massive overhaul with our time constraints?"

"I'll work within the frame of the story," she said. "Nothing else has to change. I know your vision, and I respect it."

"It's still a lot of work. I'd have to bring you on as a partner and give you on-screen credit. That's how it works with original screenplays."

She fidgeted with a matching salt and pepper shaker set. Julian wished she didn't look so nervous. He'd agree to anything if it meant they could work together. Their long discussions into the night, debating ideas, meant something to him. That was a revelation to him. He'd been so protective of this project in the past.

"Screenplay by Julian L. Knight and Nina Taylor," he said. "Don't you like the sound of that?"

"Please don't think I'm trying to hijack your project."

"I don't," he said. "You, on the other hand, may want to overthink this. Do you *really* want your name linked to mine?"

A crease forged between her brows. "Why wouldn't I?"

Julian's gaze fell to the counter, catching the flecks of gold in the earth-toned granite. "I don't expect the critics will be lining up to applaud my efforts. They're going to trash it."

She inched closer to him. Their heads were nearly touching. "Not if it's good. They may never gush over it, but they can't trash it if it's good."

He kissed the tip of her nose. "Is it…good?"

She twisted her lips to one side. "As it is? Pretty good."

That wasn't good enough. "If we partner up, I'd have to pay you more."

"I'm not in it for money."

Julian sipped his vodka. "You're more principled than I am."

He wasn't expecting to make any money from his first film. Breaking even and a few positive reviews were the best he could hope for. He considered it an investment, a way to reset his image and establish himself as a serious filmmaker.

She took his glass from him, raised it to her lips and sipped, her expression vacant. "I went to Miami to fulfill one of my mother's dreams. Doing this sort of work fulfills one of my own."

It made sense. She loved cinema. She loved writing. Here was a chance to combine those two loves.

She took another sip and set the glass down. "You know what?"

"What?"

"I'm in it for money, too. I want to partner with you, and I want to get paid. This *is* a business."

Now they were on the same page. "I think we're going to work well together."

Her lips curled in the sort of smile she saved just for him. "How would you feel if I stuck around during production? I'd love to see the director at work."

"Is it okay if the director rests his head on your lap when he's losing his grip?"

She circled the breakfast bar and hugged him from behind, resting her cheek on the space between his shoulder blades. "Don't worry. You can do this."

"*We* can do this." Did he have to remind her that she was in this up to her teeth?

"Yeah, yeah," she said, and returned to her packing.

Julian followed her into the bathroom. It was a decent size by New York standards. It did not compare to the marble and brass sanctuary they'd left behind. There was only one sink, and the walk-in shower wouldn't fit two. It had rained earlier, and the streetlights bled into the small water-stained window.

"Are you almost done packing?" he asked.

"Nowhere close." She opened the medicine cabinet and pulled out an assortment of vials and jars. "You keep me busy, Mr. Knight."

"Would you like to stay one more night? There's no rush."

"You…wouldn't mind?"

"Not at all." Spending time away from the hotel was good for them. It took them out of the fantasy and put them squarely in real life. "Plus, I should keep an eye on Ted."

"Someone has to," she said. Earlier, she'd showed him a social media post that had them both in stitches. *Is that #JLK hauling a pink couch into my BFF's building...or am I still drunk?*

"So, it's settled."

She opened a drawer and pulled out a strip of Trojans. "Should I pack these, too?"

"Sure." Julian reached out and tugged at her T-shirt. "Consider leaving this behind, and any other of your former lovers' clothing."

"But the cotton is so soft!" she protested.

He gathered the hem of the tee and gently tugged it over her head. Her past lovers could choke on their misery. Those breasts, those hips, that body and all that soft skin were his.

She touched the tip of a finger to his chin. "I love the way you look at me."

"I'm not thinking loving thoughts," he warned.

"Good." She ripped off a condom packet from the strip. He tried to take it from her, but she was too quick. "Oh, please. Allow me."

Earlier, they'd played and teased each other. This time, Julian cut out the superfluous. His desire filled him with urgent need. He slid her thin panties down to her ankles then turned her around. She tilted forward, pressing her palms to the wall.

They really did work well together.

# Sixteen

The simplest and most pleasurable way to rouse Nina from sleep was to press kisses to the back of her knees. It was daybreak in Miami, and the lavish hotel room was cloaked in shadows. Julian leaned over Nina's sleeping body and rubbed his chin, rough with stubble, into the softness of her thigh until she stirred and lifted her head off the pillow. Her eyes shone black in the darkness. Groggy still, she extended a hand, an invitation. "Come back to bed."

He was tempted, but he had other plans for her. "Let's go for a swim."

She raised herself on one elbow. "Now?"

"Trust me. You'll like this."

She kicked back the sheets, murmuring something about being too sleepy to argue. Minutes later, she came out of the bathroom in a simple black bikini. She reached for a silk tunic draped over the back of an armchair. "Ready."

"Are you sure that's all you'll need?"

"Oh, right." She found her flip-flops and slipped them on.

"We're going to stay awhile," he said.

She went into the bathroom for a bottle of sunscreen. "Okay. Ready."

Julian crossed the room to retrieve her weekender bag hanging from a peg in the closet and tossed it to her. "You'll need a change of clothes."

"Oh!" She brightened. "You should have said so." She did a quick job of packing. "Almost done."

Julian watched as she darted from the nightstand to the writing desk. Then with a sigh of frustration, she grabbed her purse and dumped the contents on the bench at the foot of the bed.

Julian checked his watch. He wanted to head out early. "What are you looking for?"

"My…um…nothing…" Although she'd stopped fretting, her brown eyes betrayed her worry. "It's not important."

"If it's not important, forget it. Let's go!"

Pete brought the car around. Julian raised the partition between the front and back seats as he had started to do whenever Nina was in the car. Two hours later, they pulled up to mile marker thirty-three on the Overseas Highway. Julian had reserved a simple boat, a twenty-foot Sportcraft with a Bimini top. He extended a hand to help her aboard. She turned to him, her face flush with delight. "Julian, where are you taking me?"

"I'll be honest. I have no idea."

"Do you know how to drive this?"

He laughed. "Just climb aboard."

Julian didn't have a final destination in mind. He was motivated by the need to escape the hotel. They'd been back in Miami for weeks now and, in a way, Sand Castle was home. Since their return, they had fallen into an easy rhythm, starting the day with conference calls with their financiers, production team or casting agent. Afterward, they parted ways. She stayed in, chained to her writing desk, wrist braces in place. He left to scout locations, approve props or hold auditions. Evenings, after dinner, they lingered at the table. Nina would give him her honest opinion on everything from costumes to set design.

Everything was shaking into place, just as she'd said. Nina had turned in a brilliant script, elevating his basic story to a richer and more nuanced one. Bettina signed on for the part of Amanda and went so far as to recommend Pierce Alexander for the role of Luke.

"Anything you'd like to tell me about you and Pierce?" he'd asked Bettina.

"Anything you'd like to tell me about the woman you've been photographed with all over Miami?"

"I can tell you this—the rumors are true."

"You won't find any rumors about Pierce and me. We're discreet."

"I'm happy for you, Betty."

Julian was just about happy for everyone—full stop. He was a barrel of joy, his work life and private life running on all cylinders. But at the moment, he and his lady needed a break.

After they'd sailed out a mile or so, Julian chose to drop anchor over a reef bathed in turquoise waters. Nina stood on deck, taking in the view. Her black hair was in her signature braid. Tendrils broke free and played in the breeze. He slipped off the hair tie at the end and loosed the three sections. Her hair broke into cascading waves down her back. He thanked God that his camera was at hand. He asked her to stand still and snapped a few photos, although he'd never forget how she looked standing there in the fresh morning light.

She leaned over the rail. "Think we can dive off?"

"I expect you to, my little mermaid."

"I don't know if you picked up on this, but I'm not a world-class swimmer."

She stripped off her silk tunic, revealing taut toffee-brown skin. Julian dropped the camera and reached for her. He toyed with the ties of her bikini bottom. "May I?"

She slapped his hand away. "What if they see us?"

"Who?" He struggled to spot a single sign of human life in any direction.

"I don't know. Pete or some photographer lurking somewhere."

At this point, Julian couldn't just chalk her concerns to paranoia. He had taken extra precautions with this outing and had not provided Pete, or anyone, with an advance itinerary. "We've left Pete on land." He tested the clasp of the bra. "Shouldn't we free these beauties? They've been cooped up for so long. They need the sun."

She tossed her head back and laughed. Her large black sunglasses slipped out of her hair and tumbled onto the deck floor. "They're not cooped up. They're fine!"

In order to convince her, Julian would have to put skin in the game. He stepped out of his shorts and dived head-first into the water. He braced himself for the frigid bite of the Pacific, except the bay was warm and welcoming.

He broke the surface in time to catch Nina slipping off her bikini top. She dived in after him, the breeze making a sail out of her loose hair.

Julian swam over and caught up with her beneath the surface. While his hands explored her slick body, he closed his mouth on one of her tight nipples. He sucked hard until a faint plea escaped her. Then he kissed her full lips.

When he broke away, she splashed him with water. "Happy now?"

Julian turned his face up to the sun. "I may die of happiness!"

She giggled. "I love you when you're like this."

"Like what?" he asked, swimming circles around her.

"Playful, wild, sexy."

"Yeah?" What he said next surprised them both. "I think I love you, period."

Nina stared at him, blinking. Drops of water clung to her long lashes. She was stunningly beautiful. Julian took a deep breath, pacing himself before he did something crazy like propose marriage.

She swam to him and wrapped her limbs around his body like an octopus, gripping tight. He held her close and they bobbed in the water, the sun hard on their shoulders. She whispered in his ear, "You only think you do?"

Looking for a way to avoid the question, he kissed the spot where a vein pulsed at her neck.

She shivered despite the heat. "Let me know when you're sure. Okay?"

He slipped a hand into her bikini bottom. "Let me know when you're close."

They were going to do playful, wild and sexy things all day. That was the plan.

* * *

Nina was overwhelmed with emotion. When she felt like this (but when had she ever felt like this?), the impulse to write was strong. Only, she could not find her journal. It had been missing for weeks. She was pretty sure she'd left it in New York. But what to do in the meantime? She was so methodical and hated to start a new journal before filling the pages of an old one.

They stopped for a late lunch at a seafood shack. The place was nearly empty. Over conch fritters and beer, they talked awhile. When Julian left for the men's room, Nina borrowed a pen from the waitress and jotted on the back of a paper menu.

*Journal Entry*
   *It's love. It's love. It's love.*

# Seventeen

On the first day of October, Julian gathered the full cast at Sand Castle for the first read-through. With Grace's blessing, they'd taken over the hotel. She gave them permission to film a total of five scenes on-site and to use the cigar room for rehearsals and meetings through pre-production. The offer, however, wasn't without conditions. Frank had promised to throw a blowout wrap party on-site.

The cigar room, or Knight's Landing, as Nina called it, was fitted with a long buffet table to accommodate the cast and production staff. Julian stood at the head of the table to welcome them all. Before he uttered a word, he glanced down at Nina, seated to his right, and she nodded her encouragement. They'd been on this journey together since the start. She might be the only person in the room who saw through his mask of self-confidence, and that was saying something considering an ex-girlfriend was present.

Julian cleared his throat. "Everyone, welcome to our first table read."

The cinematographer, who had flown in from New Hampshire a few days early to "get some fishing in," raised his hand. Eyeing the custom humidors built into the walls, he said, "Will you be handing out cigars at the end of the day?"

Everyone laughed, and the ice wall of tension rising in him shattered. Every person at the table was a seasoned professional. If he could trust them and the process—if he could trust himself—things might work out.

"My writing partner, Nina, and I have a clear vision for this film, and we hope it's one you share. We've labored over every word and, for that reason, I ask that you keep to the script as much as possible. Outside that, as a director, I'm interested in the choices you'll make to bring these characters to life. Pierce, thank you for playing our charismatic con man. You're the man for the job." More laughter erupted. "And, Bettina…" Julian turned to face the woman who had shaped his past and who had a role in his future. But no sooner than he'd said her name, the general mood flattened. It was all the proof he needed to confirm his suspicions. Everyone, excluding Nina, doubted they could work together. He had to address those doubts head-on. "There's no one else I would have wanted to play Amanda. You were my first and only choice. I thank you for trusting me."

All eyes were on Bettina now. She never wasted an opportunity to shine. Addressing the room, she said, "Guys, you may not know this, but Julian and I have a bit of history." Her words were met with the low rumble of laughter. "I can vouch for him. We're in capable hands. Plus we've got a great script. And let's be honest, shooting in Miami isn't exactly a hardship. So, let's do this. Okay?"

Julian met and kept her gaze for a brief moment, hoping to communicate his gratitude. She lowered her eyes and studied her impeccably manicured nails, code that she was ready to move on. Julian clasped his hands together. "We've got twenty-eight days to wrap this up. Let's do this."

He lowered himself in his seat and straightaway reached for Nina's hand under the table. She mingled her fingers with his. As things stood, Julian was hopeful that he and Bettina would crack on and get the job done. But he was certain that he and Nina had a future.

Julian flipped open his copy of the script. "'Day. Pool. Amanda floats on her back. The man who spent the night approaches, fully dressed, and tells her that he's leaving. Amanda swims to the pool's edge.'"

The actor read his lines. "'Gotta go, babe. Let's do this again soon.'"

Bettina read hers with the perfect mix of flirtatiousness and arrogance. "'But not too soon. Okay?'"

At the first break, Nina had excused herself and left the room. When she didn't return, Julian delayed starting up again and went after her. Something about her rod-stiff posture when she'd walked out made him worry. He found her sitting alone in the garden, silently sobbing. He rushed to her.

"What's the matter, love?" he said, kneeling before her. "Why are you crying?"

She spoke through her hands. "I'm not crying."

"Then what's all this?"

"I don't know."

He pried her hands away from her face and lifted her chin to inspect her face. Her brown eyes were dry, but he wasn't reassured. She might not be crying, but she certainly was trembling. He cupped her face and kissed her eyelids. Her eyelashes fluttered against his lips.

"Tell me what's wrong," he whispered.

"That was a lot," she said.

"The table read? You don't think it's going well?"

"No!" She wrapped her arms around his neck. "It's going great, better than I could have imagined."

He stroked her hair. "Then what is it?"

"I've never experienced anything like this," she said. "A lot of the time it's just me alone with my computer and the voices in my head. Today it felt like I belonged to something, and I...don't know."

"Oh, love. Come here." He gathered her trembling body in his arms. He'd never seen her this way, and it tore him up. "You belong."

She belonged to him, but he couldn't say that without freaking her out.

"Sorry." She extracted herself from his embrace. "I didn't expect to get so emotional."

"Don't worry. I understand."

He pulled her up to her feet. She looked up at him, a glint of pride in her yes. "You were good in there," she said. "Really good."

"I may just be the next Scorsese."

"Oh, God! Help me!"

She was her playful self again, and Julian exhaled with relief. His world had spun off its axis just now. He didn't care if he had a room full of people waiting—he would have taken all the time in the world to get her to smile again.

She raised herself on the tips of her toes and kissed him. "Thank you."

"No, love, no." Julian buried his face in her hair. She smelled sweeter than any flower in the garden. "Thank you. Thank you. Thank you."

# Eighteen

A mid-October tropical storm caused *Midnight Sun* to wrap a day late. But once Julian had called it a wrap late on a Thursday afternoon, it was a party. The cast, crew and friends they'd made during the shoot gathered by the pool. The hotel staff was prepared, marching out with minibottles of Piper-Heidsieck fitted with straws and cigars for anyone who cared to smoke. The rollout happened under Grace's hawkish eye, her mouth gathered in a tight frown.

Nina approached her. "You must be happy to have us out of your hair soon."

Julian had booked the entire hotel, filling every room with the cast and heads of each creative department in order to have the privacy and freedom needed to film. Pretty soon the caravan would clear out. Nina was feeling anxious about it. She and Julian had not discussed the future. They'd been too busy. During filming, she'd stepped in as the script manager, making sure the actors kept to their lines and monitoring for lapses in continuity. This had given her a front seat to all the action. It had been an exhilarating experience, but it was over. So now what?

"Not really," Grace said.

"Are you saying you'll miss us?" Nina exclaimed. "Don't get sentimental on me now!"

"I would never." She folded her arms across her chest. "I'm nearing the end of an era. It's going to be an adjustment."

Nina felt sure there was more Grace wanted to say, but she was trapped in her role of mistress of the manor. "Come with me."

Grace slipped her a sharp glance. "Where to?"

"Let's go for a walk."

"Impossible. I'm working."

"This place runs itself. Come out for a walk with me. When was the last time you've been to the beach? And it's just across the street!"

Grace grunted, and Nina took it as a yes. She swiped two minibottles of champagne off a tray, threaded an arm around Grace's and dragged her all the way to the front gates.

"We'll be right back," Nina said to the guards.

"And if we're not, send for me," Grace added.

As soon as they made it across Ocean Drive, Grace Guzman loosened up. She slipped off her tailored cherry-red jacket. Nina had no trouble convincing her to kick off her stilettos, and together they trekked across the sand toward the shore. It was sunset, and the surf roared at their feet.

"Give me that bottle," Grace said.

"Yes, ma'am." Nina handed her a minibottle and raised her own. "Cheers?"

"I have nothing to be cheery about," she said flatly. *"¡Salud!"*

Nina decided to ask the question that had been burning inside her for months now. "Exactly what is your problem?"

"Men are my problem," she said. "My divorce is final, and my father has decided to sell the hotel."

"You're selling the Sand Castle?" Nina cried. "Why?"

"We love it, but it's a money pit. I'm going to have a hard time letting go."

So much made sense now. The way they'd catered to Julian *and* his cast *and* his crew *and* tolerated the imposed inconvenience of hours of filming, it all finally made sense. No wonder she'd kicked Nina out of the Oasis the instant a Hollywood star came calling. The hotel needed the business.

"Sorry about the divorce," Nina said, ashamed for having skipped over such a seismic life event in the first place.

"Actually, I'll drink to that." Grace raised her bottle. "Cheers!"

"That's the spirit." She wished that she and Grace had met under different circumstances. They might've become friends. She had one more question. She was pushing it, but the bubbly made her bold. "Do you think you and Francisco Cortes could be a thing?"

"I don't need a *thing*," Grace said. "Not right now."

"But you could use some company," Nina said. "Who will drink with you in the garden when I'm gone?"

"How about you and Mr. Knight?"

"What about us?" She turned to face the ocean. So much for being bold.

"I'm sorry. As a rule, I don't comment on the hotel guests' private affairs."

"It's okay. That's why I brought you out here. You can forget your rules."

"I'll say this—people come to Miami to fool around. It rarely means anything. Usually, it ends with regret."

The truth roared in Nina's ears as loud as the surf. She and Julian were not fooling around. If their affair ended tomorrow, she would not regret one sun-filled day, one night spent in his arms. But she did not want it to end. Today was particularly tough, because what were they celebrating if not the end?

"Now I've made you cry!" Grace cursed. "I should have stuck to the rules."

"Am I crying?" Nina wiped her cheeks with the back of her hand.

"I was going to say that you two look like the real deal. I've seen enough nonsense to know the difference."

Hope crashed into Nina with the force of the waves. Validation from an impartial and dispassionate observer such as Grace was priceless. It meant that she hadn't imagined this grand love affair. It wasn't all in her head. And what a relief! She was so in love with Julian, so wildly in love with him, she could not stand to lose him.

Nina couldn't overthink her present predicament. Grace was smiling at her, and it was distracting as hell. It was the first time the woman had smiled at her with genuine warmth, and it was luminous. If she weren't careful, she might fall in love with Grace.

When they got back to Sand Castle, she and Grace parted ways. The manager hurried off to her office, and

Nina set out to find Julian. The party was unraveling. Bettina and Pierce had slipped away earlier with a bottle of champagne. Everyone else was slumped on lounge beds, partied out. Julian, however, had not lost steam. He stood with a foot propped up on a chair, telling a story to a captive audience. Seeing him this loose and animated made her realize just how much pressure he must have been under these past months.

She approached, and he drew her close and dipped her into a mock Hollywood kiss. Nina played along, swooning like a screen siren. Then he gazed into her eyes. "I think we're done here."

Nina knew what he meant, but wished he'd phrased it differently. She didn't protest when he carried her off to the elevator.

"To think I hated this tin can when I first got here," he said. "Look how handy it's been. Do you remember the first time we did this?"

"I coughed up on your shirt."

"And I was completely charmed." He squeezed her tighter. "It must be this house. It has powers."

"Grace's family will be selling it soon. Maybe you should buy, rename the place Knight's Landing."

"I love this house, but I don't ever want to be here without you."

The elevator stopped, and the doors slid open. Julian carried her to the door, over the threshold and into the bedroom. He dropped her unceremoniously on the bed and plopped down alongside her. He would break any bed he owned; Nina was sure of it.

Nina rolled onto her side and raked her fingers through his hair. Eyes shut, expression soft, his profile remained strong and defined—the not-so-classic matinee idol. She was not a performer, but she would gladly play the role of his screen siren. There really wasn't much she wouldn't do for him. That included tossing her pride aside and opening up to him. "I have to tell you something."

Eyes closed, he said, "What's that, love?"

Nina called to the angels of the fresco for strength one last time. "I may be in love with you."

He slid her a look, eyes brimming with equal parts affection and amusement. She'd hedged and he knew it. "Want to tell me when you're sure?"

Her answer was buried somewhere deep in her kiss.

# Nineteen

What was next for them?

The question kept Julian up well after Nina had fallen asleep, her cheek pressed to his chest. When she breathed, her breasts pressed into his ribs. Gradually his breathing synced with hers. In every way they were one, except they lived on opposite coasts.

Last night they'd cleared one hurdle—their feelings for each other were more or less clear. Where were they going to live? He was making plans to return to California in a week to get on with editing. Would she come? Maybe she could be persuaded to fly out with him. She could write anywhere; wasn't that what she'd said? His house on the Hills wasn't as romantic as this old mansion that had become their home, but it offered plenty of space for her to spread out pages on the floor, and the view from his desk was inspiring.

Julian's phone buzzed on the nightstand, and the screen glowed green in the night. He ignored it. He was too comfortable, and he didn't want to wake Nina. Then the damn thing buzzed again and again and again. Nina moaned in her sleep and rolled onto her back. He snatched the phone and tapped on the screen to silence it. It was two in the morning, and he had a missed call from his publicist and five text messages from Kat.

Julian tossed back the duvet and swung his legs over the edge of the bed, his insides twisting with apprehension. He'd been on a high! Wrapping the movie on time if not on budget, earning the respect of the actors and the crew, collaborating with Frank—these were all things he was proud of. Getting to share the experience with the woman he loved was a surprise gift that he wasn't sure he deserved. He was willing to go to the ends to defend this newfound happiness. He remembered his life before, and he wasn't going back.

He took the phone into the bathroom, and instead of wasting time scrolling through the messages, he called Kat. She answered straightaway.

"Hey. What's going on?"

"Didn't you read my texts?"

"No. I was asleep."

"Is *she* with you?"

It was too late to play these games. "What are you getting at?"

"We need to speak privately."

"It's all clear, just talk to me."

"All right. Nina Taylor kept detailed notes of your time together. Were you aware?"

"She's a writer."

"Intimate notes, Julian."

He breathed out through a fisted hand, forcing his brain to work. He tried coming up with the worst-case scenario. "She keeps a diary."

"To later publish as books."

"That's not why she does it."

Nina had hated the experience of publishing a memoir—that much he knew. She was reluctant to write another. Besides, she didn't have to. Screenwriting credits on your résumé had a way of widening your options.

"I'm looking at her bio. She's a memoirist. That's it. Sure, she used to work at a magazine, but that was a long time ago."

"Why are you looking at her bio? What happened?"

His temper flared so rarely, but everything about this conversation was pissing him off.

"An excerpt of her diary was published on Celebrity-Soup.com."

He processed this, the gears of his brain grinding painfully slowly. "How did it get out?"

"No one knows for sure, but I need you to consider that she leaked it."

"She didn't."

"How do you know?"

"I know."

An excerpt of her diary had been published on a gossip site. That was all they knew so far. But Julian knew how this worked. They would need someone to blame, someone to cast as a villain.

"Julian, you don't know this woman. She's wiggled her way into your life, and now she's writing about it. You didn't make her sign anything. She'll probably get a book deal."

"Kat." His voice cut into the silence of the bathroom. "Be careful what you say about Nina."

"If I crossed a line, I'm sorry."

"I don't need an apology. I need you to understand that she is not some random woman who wiggled her way into anything."

He'd lured Nina into his world, a world populated with paparazzi and gossip columnists. He would shield her anyway he could. She wasn't an attention seeker. She was a writer, a thinker and a private person. He would not let anyone insult or degrade her.

"Read the excerpt and see for yourself," Kat said. "I sent you the link."

"Thanks, Kat," he mumbled. "Sorry I jumped down your throat."

"Let's talk again in the morning with cooler heads."

Julian ended the call. He scrolled his messages until he found the link to the website post. The title alone turned his stomach sour. *One Hot Knight in Miami.* Once again, his private life was served up for entertainment. He scrolled down and started reading. The words jumped at him. *"May I taste?"* Julian heard the tap on the bathroom door, but he couldn't stop reading. *When his tongue meets my tender skin, I'm not prepared for the rush... We haven't made it to the bed.*

Intimate details.

# Twenty

Nina was alone in bed. She was sure of it even before she opened her eyes to heavy darkness. Julian was in the bathroom arguing with someone over the phone. When silence settled in, she slipped out of bed and tapped on the bathroom door. No answer. She called out his name. Nothing. She opened the door a crack. "Everything okay?"

He was staring intently at his phone, and when he looked up at her, the glow from the small screen gave him an eerie look.

"Julian, what's the matter?"

He handed her the phone. "Explain this to me."

"Explain what?"

She glanced at the screen, more concerned with the tight set of his jaw than any clandestine photo or provocative tweet. But she recognized the words as her own. *He presses me against the door and hunches low.* "What's this?"

"An excerpt from your journal."

Nina felt a tightening in her gut. She was going to be sick.

"How did it end up online?" he asked.

"I don't know!" she cried. "You tell me!"

"Did you leak it?" Those four words sent Nina reeling. She smacked his phone onto the counter and backed out of the doorway. He followed her into the bedroom. His voice was low when he asked the follow-up question. "Did they pay you?"

Each word was a blow, and he wouldn't shut up.

"I need to hear you say it. Then we'll figure out what to do."

She switched on the lights in the bedroom to better confront him. "You think I sold our story for money?"

"I don't. But since we don't have a confidentiality agreement, I have to ask."

"A confidentiality agreement?"

"I know. It sounds terrible, but it's more common than you'd think."

On the first day they'd met, they'd hashed out an agreement. She'd promised not to write about him or anything that happened between them. She reminded him of her promise. His silence told her that it wasn't enough. There was nothing he could add to or subtract from the equation to change the value of this revelation. Her promise, her *word*, was not enough.

Alarm bells were ringing in the back of her head. She would not waste her breath trying to reassure Julian. She had to look out for herself. Someone had stolen her diary. How did they get it? Who had it now? How many people were reading, sharing and tweeting her words at this moment?

She paced around the room. Soon Julian was doing the same. They circled each other.

"Where's the notebook?" he said. "Let's see it."

She opened the nightstand and desk drawers, hoping her journal would magically appear. "It's not here. To be honest, it's been missing for weeks."

He faced her. "Your notebook is missing? And you said nothing?"

"I asked the front desk if anyone had returned a missing journal. To be honest, I figured it would turn up."

"Let me understand. You kept a detailed record of everything we said and did together and took no measures to protect it?"

Her breath was coming hard and fast. Legal agreements and records... Who was this man? "We're talking about a *diary*, a place for my private thoughts. With or without any mention of you, I would have protected it. My diaries are private. I don't share them with anyone."

"Except you do," he said. "You turn them into books."

Nina's anger snapped. "Get out."

"Calm down. We can talk this through."

"I *am* calm. And I want you out."

"Where do you want me to go? It's the middle of the night."

"There's a pullout couch in the other room," she said. "Don't worry. It's comfortable."

Julian leaned against a chest of drawers. He'd gone pale under his honey-brown complexion. Nina turned away. Although he had hurt her, she could not bear to see him in pain. This was their first fight, and each blow had proven to be fatal.

* * *

The Uber driver hummed to the tune on the radio. John Legend was crooning about everlasting love over the speakers. Nina wished she could rip the radio out of the dashboard and toss it out the window. She was living proof that love was dead.

"How far is it?" she asked.

"It's way out by the zoo, so…yeah."

This meant nothing to Nina. "Okay."

"Good thing the roads are clear."

It was five in the morning. Nina had been up all night. With Julian banished to the other room, she packed, disentangled her phone charger from his and stuffed her makeup and important things in her tote bag. A quick text to Valerie and she had someplace to crash until she figured out her next step. The important thing was to slip out of Sand Castle undetected. She'd left Julian a note. It didn't say much.

The driver tapped her fingers on the steering wheel. She had long, elegant fingers and wore a princess-cut diamond on her left hand. Maybe love wasn't dead after all. She glanced at Nina and suggested she take a nap. It was a tempting suggestion, but bad things happened when passengers dozed off in public transportation. However, pretending to nap meant that the driver could go back to humming love songs and Nina could fold into herself and mope undisturbed.

She reclined her seat but did not close her eyes. If she did, she'd relive the night's events. She kept her eyes locked on the tangled ribbon of highway. The minutes ticked away, and her eyes went dry from the strain. Despite her efforts, the unwelcome memories surfaced anyway and she relived it all.

* * *

It was close to six when Nina arrived at her cousin's town house. Valerie lived with her husband in a tidy gated community. The porch lights were on, and she was waiting at the door. Valerie inspected her, eyes wide with concern. "Are you okay?" she asked. "What happened?"

"We had a fight. It's over."

"It's over after one fight?"

Nina massaged her temples. She did not want to be rude, but she really did not want to talk about it.

"You look exhausted," Valerie said. "I'll take you upstairs."

The guest bedroom was, funny enough, a home office with a daybed pushed up against a wall. Nina stumbled onto the bed, and the enormity of what she'd lost came crushing on her. She wanted to howl with grief, but Valerie, in her pajamas and fuzzy slippers, hair tied back with a silk scarf, kept shuffling in and out of the room. She brought in a glass of water, a bottle of painkillers and a weighted blanket. Her cousin was an excellent hostess.

"Get some sleep," she said. "I took the day off. We can talk later."

"Why are you so nice?"

Valerie paused, a hand on the doorknob. "Excuse me?"

Nina sat up. "I've been nothing but standoffish with you…even bitchy. I keep hoping you'll take the hint, and you never do."

Valerie's face crumpled. Without makeup, she looked far younger than her twenty-nine years. "It's a long story."

Nina shrugged. "I'd like to hear it."

Valerie shut the door and took a seat at the neat Ikea desk. Nina had instantly recognized it. She'd had a similar one a few years back. "My favorite uncle, *your* father, died when I was seven."

Nina was nine when her father had died in a car wreck. She hadn't known that her absentee parent was anyone's favorite anything. She hadn't known much about him period. Her mother had been in her thirties when she got pregnant and not at all interested in settling down.

"On the drive back from the funeral, my parents were talking. They said he'd wasted his life. He was handsome and charming—a so-called ladies' man. But as you know, he never worked a day in his life."

"Yeah. I heard." Nina looked down at her knuckles, embarrassed on her cousin's behalf. Her father's inability to hold a job was one of the reasons her mother had refused to take him seriously. When Nina was old enough, she'd explained that her father had been a fling and nothing more. "Someone to have a good time with."

"It was the first time, at least to my recollection, that my parents ever mentioned you by name. My cousin Nina."

Nina's heart filled with a sort of ache that she had long thought extinct. Why did she have to pry? What good was it to revive these old ghosts?

"My mom went on and on about how beautiful you were. My dad thought my uncle was a loser for not raising his daughter. According to my folks, he didn't like to be around your mom because they'd fight—"

"About money," Nina blurted. "Yeah. I know."

It was true her parents had fought about money, late child support payments in particular. Then her dad had died prematurely, leaving her mother to make do. Although money was tight, Nina had not wanted for anything—ever. And by the time she'd started middle school, her mother's career had picked up. "Do you pity me? Is that it?"

"Oh, no! It's the opposite!" Valerie moved off the chair and onto the daybed next to Nina. "My parents talked about you like some beautiful girl in New York City. In my mind, you were Eloise living at the Plaza. I wanted us to be best friends."

Nina pressed a palm to her forehead. For her, it had been the opposite experience. Her father's big, boisterous family, with their Caribbean accents and traditions and foods, were an exclusive club to which she'd been barred access. She had never wanted to have anything to do with them. Valerie shuffled out of the room and returned with a box of tissues.

"Where are your parents now?" Nina asked.

"Port-au-Prince. They live there six months out of the year."

The older generation was now out of the picture. Here was Valerie, singlehandedly trying to repair the past and reshape the future. Nina couldn't let her do it alone. "Thanks for the tissues. I'm going to wallow now."

"Gotcha." Valerie rose to her feet. The sound of water rushing through pipes made the town house hum. Valerie's husband was likely getting ready for work. What was his name again? Oh, yes. Patrick. "The weighted blanket will help with that. It's a comfort. Trust me."

Nina wondered what Valerie would have to wallow about then stopped herself before she went down that route once again. She'd made that mistake with Grace.

Everybody, no matter how rich, successful, stylish and attractive, had something to wallow about.

After Valerie left, Nina crawled under the blanket with the box of tissues, wholly determined to soak the pillows with tears.

Nina stayed through the weekend, which meant she spent two days in her blanket fort, wiping tears and blowing her nose into wads of tissue. It helped that in her haste to escape the hotel, she'd inadvertently grabbed one of Julian's T-shirts. She clung to it like Linus to a blanket. Now and again, she raised it to her nose, inhaling his clean scent, and she was in his arms again. Everything she loved about him surrounding her, except his massive trust issues and his disloyal little heart.

She was caught in an infinity loop of heartache and humiliation. It was one thing to have her heart broken and yet another to be exposed to public ridicule at the same time. The one person who could possibly understand was the jerk who'd smashed her heart in the first place.

On Sunday, Nina had no choice but to crawl out of her cave. It was Patrick's thirty-fifth birthday, and Valerie had organized a little gathering. Since Nina had been hiding out in the man's home office for days, she figured she owed it to him to shower, dress, brush her hair and wish him a happy birthday. In the morning, she was flying back to New York.

At the moment, she had a few more solid hours of blanket-fort time ahead. She wiggled around and settled in. Just as she got comfortable, Valerie burst into her room, carrying a laptop.

"Julian made a statement. Check this out."

Nina's heart took off in wild gallop. He'd made a statement! What was there to say? She shoved off the blanket and joined Valerie at the desk. Her cousin was clicking around the web, trying to pull up a *Miami Herald* article without first having to subscribe to the paper, join an email list or take a survey.

"Okay. Here goes… Wait. Okay. Damn it! Buffering."

A video was downloading at a snail's pace. Nina watched the screen in terror. The slow Wi-Fi was criminal, but as much as she was eager for the video to load, she wasn't prepared to see Julian again—not even on a computer screen.

"Has he tried to reach out to you?" Valerie asked while they waited.

That was anyone's guess. "I haven't checked my phone."

She'd left it on airplane mode and buried it in the bottom of a bag. Nina had needed to go dark. She could not handle the onslaught of messages that had flooded her inboxes. Her social media mentions had exploded. Last she'd checked her phone, #1HOTKNIGHT and #1KNIGHTSTAND were trending and every troll in the world agreed that she stood to gain the most from the scandal. After her agent had called with an offer from an editor to buy the rights to the "hot Knight story," she'd had no choice but to go dark.

"Okay. Here we go!" Valerie said.

A brief intro and there he was, standing in the hotel's courtyard. The fountain splashed and gurgled just a few feet away. He wore his usual T-shirt and tailored jacket combo, eyes hidden behind sunglasses.

Nina yearned for him. She couldn't help it. The sight of him would always move her this way.

"We're here today in Miami Beach with actor JL Knight," the reporter said. "Mr. Knight, you are certainly no stranger to scandal. Let's get to the heart of it. Who is Nina Taylor? Did you know her long?"

Julian looked straight to camera to deliver his answer. "Nina Taylor is an acquaintance, someone that I met and worked with here in Miami. The publication of her diary was a violation of privacy. We will pursue legal action."

"Thank you, Mr. Knight."

End of video.

Nina edged Valerie aside and refreshed the web page. "Is that it? That can't be it."

"That's it," Valerie said.

"An acquaintance?" Nina uttered. "Did he just call me an acquaintance?"

Valerie dismissed this. "His publicist probably drafted that statement. A lot of celebrities have their publicists handle their breakups. It's less complicated that way."

The room expanded and contracted around Nina. Julian's statement was factually accurate. They were acquaintances. They'd met and worked together in Miami. They'd kissed in the moonlight, napped in the sun, swum naked in the bay and made love through the night, but that didn't change the facts. If she'd been anything more than an acquaintance, he would have known that she could have never betrayed him for professional advancement.

"Here's my take," Valerie said. "This was damage control. Nothing more."

Nina left the room and stumbled down the hall to the bathroom. Julian would have called her on this—she did have a habit of hiding out in bathrooms—but she couldn't count on Julian to save her from herself anymore. He was an acquaintance. Someone that she'd met and worked with in Miami. Nothing more.

# Twenty-One

By four in the afternoon, the two-story town house was filled with the scent of fried onions, fried plantains and fried pork. Valerie's mother-in-law and other close family members had arrived early to help out in the kitchen and set up for the party. Nina's bedroom window overlooked the back patio. Patrick and his friends gathered there, nursing glasses of amber liquor or bottles of beer. Laughter, chatter and riotous *kompa* music drifted to the second floor.

Nina looked longingly down at the tableau. This was everything that she had been deprived of growing up. She had long wished to belong to a clan of some sort. And this was without a doubt a gathering of a clan. Valerie was extending an invitation, but was it too late?

*Do I fit in?*

She was itching to reach for a pen and write the words

down. The sad thing was, she didn't trust herself with a journal—not anymore. Julian was right about one point. When it suited her, when it was convenient, she *did* sell her private thoughts for profit. If she hadn't given in to the childish need to "Dear Diary" every life event, she could have spared herself a lot of pain over the years.

Valerie brought her a cup of tea. "I told *ma belle-mère* that you had a migraine and, she sent up ginger tea. She doesn't believe in pills. It's only weird because she's a pharmacist."

Nina set the hot cup of tea on the windowsill. "Give me a sec and I'll head down with you. I'm starting to feel like the disturbed woman in the attic up here by myself."

Nina studied her reflection in her compact mirror and winced. She swiped on lip gloss to liven up her complexion, but that was a lot to expect from a fifteen-dollar tube of goo. The doorbell rang and, a moment later, a child let out a bloodcurdling scream. Nina startled and dropped the lip gloss wand. Next thing, she and Valerie had joined a stampede toward the front door. They rushed down the stairs but only made it as far as the landing. The foyer was cramped, everyone straining to catch a glimpse at whoever was on the other side of the screen door. There was one word on everybody's lips: *"Thunder!"*

Nina wished a bolt of lightning would strike her dead.

Valerie turned to her, eyes bright. "It's Julian!"

Nina gripped her cousin's arm. "How did he know where to find me?"

"I don't know!"

The birthday boy, already a little drunk, had some

insight. "He called the house and asked if he could come by!"

"And you said yes?" Nina said.

Patrick was a smart, attractive man. He had a quick smile and poreless chocolate-brown skin. Otherwise, he was a guy's guy and proved it with his next words. "JL Knight calls and says he wants to come over on my birthday and you expect me to say no? Get outta here!"

"He's not here to see you!" Valerie scoffed and turned to Nina. "Don't look so grim. He's probably here to grovel."

"I don't want him to grovel."

The look her cousin gave her left no room for misinterpretation. "Now I know you're full of it."

"It won't change anything."

"It's a start," Valerie said. "He grovels a bit, and then you work something out, come to an understanding."

Valerie's mother-in-law came out of the kitchen brandishing a massive wooden pestle. She elbowed her way through the crowd and proceeded to question the intruder. Nina ordered Patrick to call back his mother. She didn't want Julian pummeled to death with a wooden pestle. Her concern amused Valerie. "Let the groveling begin!"

If he groveled, they could work something out, come to an understanding. That was the rule. Except Julian wasn't groveling, not even a little bit.

Valerie had finally let him in, apologizing for the raucous welcome. "Sorry! My family is extra." And there he was, standing in the tight foyer, looming over everyone, her tall, dark and handsome movie star.

After Patrick gushed over him and they snapped the

obligatory photo, Valerie led them to a quiet seating area on the second floor so they could talk in peace. They settled on opposite ends of an upholstered bench. He looked like a dream in a blue button-down shirt, his hair slicked back. He had no right to look so good when she felt and looked as if she were living a nightmare.

"Sorry for crashing your party," he said to Valerie.

"Don't be ridiculous," Valerie said smoothly. "You've made my husband's year. Anything to eat or drink? We've got plenty of food."

"No. Thank you," Julian said. "I won't be staying long."

He wasn't staying long. Drive-by groveling? Did that count for anything?

"Let me know if you change your mind," Valerie said.

Nina's gaze stayed with Valerie as she headed down the stairs. What she would give if her cousin could stay and arbitrate. Julian was as stiff as a stick figure. He sat tilted forward, elbows on knees and fingers in a steeple under his chin. Silence pulsed around them. She felt sure it echoed the beat of her heart.

"How are you doing?" he asked.

"I'm flying home tomorrow." That wasn't the answer to his question, but that was all she had to say.

He nodded as if processing her words. Then he very slowly opened the messenger bag that he'd dropped at his feet and pulled out her journal. The pages were waterlogged and the red leather cover had new scuff marks.

Relief shot through her. "Oh, God! Where did you find it?"

"Grace found it in the garden." He flipped it open. "Someone ripped out a few pages before tossing it in the bushes."

He handed her the journal. She opened it on her lap

and ran her finger along the frayed edges of the missing pages. "What sort of person does this?"

"The sort of person that is Pete. He was caught on camera."

Nausea rolled through her. "I *warned* you about him."

"I know," he said quietly. "And I'm sorry. That's why I'm here. I could have had it shipped to you, but I needed to look you in the eye and tell you how sorry I am. Pete was working with that website, feeding them information and tipping off their photographers, and I overlooked the obvious signs. I just didn't want to cost a working man his job if it wasn't true."

Did this count as groveling? Nina wasn't sure.

"The only reason they did this to you was to get to me," he said. "They used you, and I'm sorry for the hurt and embarrassment."

*They* may have caused her great embarrassment; only *he* had hurt her.

Nina tightened her grip on the journal. "I saw your statement. I don't want to take legal action. I just want this story to go away."

"I understand."

He rose from the bench and picked up the bag. "If I have any more information, can I call you? Will you answer?"

Nina swallowed past the pit in her throat and nodded. He stared at her awhile, looking as if he had more to say but finally deciding against it. "Okay, Nina. Take care."

She nodded again and turned to stare at a framed painting of a rowboat. She could not bear to watch him leave.

# Twenty-Two

After Julian made a discreet exit, Valerie joined her upstairs. "How did it go?"

Nina struggled to come up with an answer that simple question. "He didn't grovel."

Valerie plopped down on the bench next to her. "Maybe your standards are too high. Nobody said he had to bend the knee."

"An apology would have been nice."

"He didn't apologize? For anything?"

"He said he was sorry."

"Okay. That sounds like an apology."

"But it wasn't!" Nina blinked, her tears near. "He apologized for the wrong thing."

Valerie looked genuinely confused. "You're not making sense."

"He kept going on about what *they*'d done to me. The

driver who stole my diary...the website that published it. It was all their fault. He was sorry that *they* hurt me."

The light in Valerie's eyes dimmed as her hopes for a happy ending died. "He doesn't get it."

"No! He doesn't!" Nina cried, but she was happy that her cousin did.

The next day, Nina flew home. She sat cramped in a middle seat, staring at the minuscule television screen. Meg Ryan was falling in love (again) with Tom Hanks. The actress opened wide blue eyes, filled with hope, and Nina wanted to punch the screen. The journal on her lap wasn't the one Julian had returned. As a parting gift, Valerie had unearthed her father's notebooks and offered them to her in a bundle wrapped in ribbon. Each notebook was inscribed with his name in ink: Raymond Pierre. Nina treasured them. She was not a fool for filling up diaries; she was carrying on a family tradition.

It was a relief to return to her quiet apartment. And it did not take long for her to resume her quiet life with its routines: mornings at the gym, writing sprints, cooking, some television and on occasion drinks with Laetitia. It was the best she could stitch together. She'd been banned from the creative carnival of which Julian was the center. So now she lived the low-key life of an exile. Her sleepless nights were more comfortable in her own bed, but her sense of loss did not lessen with time. Most mornings, she woke up confused to find that Julian wasn't within arm's reach. Then she'd go on with her day, her heart heavy, as if filled with slush. At night, she missed his overwhelming presence, the way he filled whatever bedroom they shared with laughter. She missed the sound of his voice.

And days stretched into weeks.

The paperback edition of her memoir steadily climbed the bestseller lists. Requests for interviews and appearances poured in. Only now she was known as *that* Nina Taylor—a virtually unknown author whose career had skyrocketed after she slept with an action star and wrote about it. To the dismay of her publisher, she turned down every interview request, but that only seemed to add to her mystique.

She had no idea how Julian was doing, and that was a sort of torture. The one time she'd googled him, she'd stumbled upon this gem: *If you thought JLK was a "Wham! Bam!" type of lover, think again! Diary excerpts paint a portrait of a sensitive and intuitive man. Men and women alike are clamoring for a piece of that action. The actor could not be reached for comment.*

On a chilly Saturday morning in January, Nina and Laetitia, bundled in parkas, trekked back home from spin class. They spotted a woman on their stoop, frantically pressing the buzzer.

"Looks like there's going to be some drama!" Laetitia said.

"Bet you anything that it's Carl in 3F," Nina said. "He's so messy."

"I know! Right?"

Laetitia sprinted forward. She was a decade older than Nina. Her sloppy breakup with Ted (an episode only referred to as TEDx) had done her good. Aggressive self-care was working wonders. Her inky-black hair was glossy and her olive complexion glowed. She was

once again her upbeat self—and as nosy as ever. She
hopped up the steps, pausing on the landing to peek over
the woman's shoulder. Nina caught her friend's startled
expression and stopped to study the petite blonde more
closely. She suddenly looked uncannily familiar.

"Don't waste your time," Laetitia said. "No one is
in 3D."

The woman whirled to face Laetitia. "Why? Did she
move out?"

"Depends. Who's asking?"

"Katia Wells," she replied. "I'm looking for Nina Taylor. Do you know where she is?"

"I'm right here."

She narrowed her eyes at Nina. "Ah! There you are.
That's a relief!"

Nina's body stiffened under the down-filled parka,
and it had nothing to do with the biting chill in the air.
"Is Julian with you?"

"No. Just me," she said. "Is this a bad time? I hoped
we could grab coffee."

Moments later, Nina sat across from Katia at a
bar-height table at a Starbucks, stirring sugar into an
almond-milk macchiato. Katia lifted the lid of her cup
and blew on the foam, in no apparent hurry to explain
herself. Why had she shown up at her door? What was
so urgent? Had Julian sent her?

"I owe you an apology," Katia said.

That was not what Nina expected to hear. As far as
she knew, she had no beef with Katia Wells. "What for?"

"I misjudged you," she said. "I thought you'd leaked
your diary. I was sure of it."

Not. This. Again. "Why would I do that?"

"Why do people do anything?" Katia fit the lid over the rim of her cup with a snap. "For money or attention or both."

This was absurd. Who, in their right mind, would want this kind of attention?

"You had your chance to capitalize on the scandal, and you didn't," Katia said. "No talk-show interviews. No book deals."

Nina grabbed a packet of sugar and squeezed it between her palms. "You didn't have to fly across the country to tell me that. I'm sure there's a Hallmark card that fits the bill."

"I didn't fly across the country to apologize. Thought it would be a nice way to break the ice, that's all."

Nina had ice in her veins. There wasn't much Katia could say to warm her disposition. Plus, she wasn't the finest of diplomats; it was time this woman got to the point. "Did Julian send you?"

"No!" Katia was emphatic. "He doesn't know I'm here."

Nina prayed disappointment wasn't oozing from her pores. Julian hadn't sent her because Julian had moved on. If she could only accept that maybe she could move on as well.

"As the head of publicity for Knight Films, I'm here to set up press for the New York premiere in April."

Nina couldn't suppress a jolt of excitement. "A premiere? Already?"

"Yup! It's an exciting time for us. *Midnight Sun* is getting good buzz. We've decided on a limited release— New York and LA."

Nina had flinched at Katia's use of the collective *us*

and *we*, and now she was desperate to end this meeting. "What do you want from me, exactly?"

Katia took a long sip of her soy latte, a reminder that Nina's macchiato was cooling fast. "I'm here to coax you out of hiding."

"Coax me out of what?"

"Hiding," Katia said. "Here's how I see it. You're a woman, and you're sexual. You wrote about a meaningful encounter with a man. There's no shame in that."

"You make it sound like I'm cowering in shame. I'm not."

Nina was very strategically staying above the fray. She wasn't making public appearances, but she wasn't sequestered in her apartment, either. She'd resumed her routines, picking up freelance editorial work and tinkering with creative projects of her own. The problem was the "routine" part. Life with Julian had been anything but mundane. Bright and fun, every day had been an indulgence.

"You are—kind of—and I can tell you it's not a good look. You should speak up."

"Why?" Just a second ago Katia was praising her for *not* speaking up. What was she missing here?

"To help the movie. Okay?" Katia spoke with caustic impatience, as if she couldn't believe she had to explain this to a seasoned professional. "Right now, this movie release is covered under your big shadow. You're the elephant in the room. You—"

"Okay. Stop." Nina couldn't hear one more cliché. "I've done my part. I've stayed away from press and—"

"And it's only made things more awkward. You need to speak up."

"You mean throw myself to the wolves."

"No one is asking for a blood sacrifice," Katia said. "Don't forget, this is your film, too. It's in your best interest to promote it."

How could she? She had a scarlet letter pinned to her lapel. "It's not a good idea."

"I get your concerns," Katia said. "But listen. The one thing I know is PR. How do you think I got this job? Up until now I was Julian's capable assistant. I had to rebrand myself, and so do you."

This conversation couldn't get more LA if they tried. "I think with time all of this will go away."

"No! You have to be proactive. Unless you want to be known as #sexgoddess for the rest of your life."

"Hashtag what?" Nina came close to knocking over her coffee. She moved her cup out of the way with a shaky hand.

"Don't you google yourself?"

"No," Nina said. "I'm not insane."

"Well, #sexgoddess is what you're known as these days. Way better than #famewhore, in my opinion."

Nina drummed the tabletop with her fingertips. "Awesome...just awesome."

"I know. It sucks. It all sucks."

It sucked that Katia was right. Nina had been hiding. She wanted nothing more than to crawl into a hole, or her apartment, and die. She'd had a hand in the making of this scandal and was deeply embarrassed about it. How could she have been so careless as to leaving her diary in a public garden? Once again, her published words had caused a loved one pain.

"Come out and support the film," Katia said. "The Miami Film Festival in March is a good place to start. You won't have to talk to the press. If you show up to the director's Q&A event, I'll make sure your photo gets to the press."

"Will Julian be there?"

"Of course. He's the director."

Nina reached for her coat hanging on the back of her chair. She was suddenly feeling cold in this hot and cramped coffee shop.

"I'm sorry things didn't work out between you two, but he's worked so hard on this. You more than anyone should know that. If you ever cared for him—"

"I love him!"

Katia grabbed the table as if a quake had hit. The words had exploded from Nina. She didn't *care* for him. She loved him. Nina loved Julian Knight, and she couldn't carry that truth around like a concealed weapon anymore. Was Julian worthy of her love? That was a separate issue.

"Sorry, Katia," she said. It wasn't fair to unload on her. "I didn't mean to scare you."

Katia raised her hands to her head and massaged her temples. "Ugh! I promised I wouldn't meddle."

"That's surprising. All you've done is meddle."

"Clearly, I'm good at it." She laughed, nervous. "I can't speak for my boss's feelings, obviously. I can say that he hasn't been the same since Miami. I've seen him low before, but this is different."

Nina didn't like the idea of Julian feeling low. A part of her was comforted by the idea that he was out in the world, making it a better place through sheer charisma and joy.

"I want to talk to him," Nina said. "Ask him to call me."

"I can't do that. He doesn't know I'm here."

Nina grabbed her keys off the table. "Fine."

"Wait!" Katia cried. "Let me see what I can do."

Katia whipped out her phone and stepped outside to place the call. Nina dropped her keys, shed off her heavy coat and finally took a sip of coffee.

# Twenty-Three

Kat called early on a Saturday morning while Julian, in the company of Wasabi, was sprawled on his couch, watching *Jules and Jim*. He was working his way down the list of Nina's favorite classic films. This was his new weekend ritual, and he was serious about it. He would have normally let voice mail pick up, except Kat was away, setting up the press junket for the New York release. This was new territory for her, and she might have questions. He didn't expect her to have a convoluted story to tell involving Nina.

After months of tortuous silence, a demand. Nina was *demanding* that he call her. As if he had to be forced into it and that he hadn't tried a thousand times. The thought of hearing her voice again...

"Alright," he said.

"You're not mad?" Kat stammered. "You asked me not to meddle, and I clearly am."

He'd write her a bonus check for this. "How about this? Don't bring it up again and I won't."

"Gotcha."

"Is she with you? May I speak with her?"

"Give it thirty minutes, okay? We're at a crowded coffee shop."

"Okay."

*Thirty minutes.* Julian lifted Wasabi off his chest and got up to shower and shave. He always wanted to look good for her, even on a call. With ten minutes left to go, he wandered out to the yard. He needed a clear head. What did she want to say to him? What would he say to her?

He and Rosie had resumed their weekly meetings at the gazebo. She thought he was wrong for letting go of the #sexgoddess—as Nina was referred to on Twitter.

"It's the best thing for her," he'd said to Rosie.

"How do you figure?"

"No one would have ripped and sold pages of her diary if she were not writing about me. I can't ignore that."

When Julian had finally cooled down and read the entire published excerpt, he was moved to tears. Her heart beat in every line. He couldn't imagine the embarrassment it must have caused her, still caused her to this day. She was a serious writer, and they'd made her a hashtag. It infuriated him that they'd reduced her to a cartoon character. That was his fault.

Rosie toyed with the plastic lighter in her hand. A weak flame blossomed then failed with each flick of her thumb. "Julian, life is not cinema."

At the mention of his name, Julian snapped to attention. To Rosie he'd always been JL Knight. This departure from the norm was remarkable. "I'm aware."

"You don't get to run around, bark orders and blow things up. You have to talk to her, and you have to listen to what she has to say." Then she added, wryly, "You're not really a knight, you know."

He could not get Rosie's words out of his head. That conversation had nudged the boulder sealing his reasons in place. Nina had walked out, but he'd stayed away to protect her privacy, dignity and reputation. That's what he told himself. Or, possibly, he'd blown it all up because it was easier that way.

With five minutes left, Julian went back inside and straight to the kitchen. He filled his trusty electric kettle, the one that he'd purchased the week he arrived in America. Soon the sound of gurgling water was the only sound. His house, his *life*, was devastatingly quiet. Julian couldn't wait a second longer. He grabbed his phone and dialed her number.

"Nina?"

"Hi."

Julian closed his eyes. Every emotion that she had ever stirred in him hit him all at once. "You wanted to speak with me."

"Yes."

Her tone was guarded, and it killed him. They'd always been so free with each other.

"It's time I write about the whole missing-diary episode."

Now this was a surprise. "Did Kat put you up to this?"

"No." The one syllable dropped in the space between them. "It's something I need to do."

"Why?" He couldn't understand. Why would she want to throw more red meat to the wolves?

"I've been silent all these months, and I want my voice back."

"I understand, but I'm worried—"

"You don't understand," she said. "I've been labeled everything from a slutty opportunist to a sex goddess. I need to define who I am."

Julian ran his palm over his face. Fearful of making a bad situation worse, he opted to shut up.

"If you think my goal is to sell more books or somehow keep this story alive—"

"I don't think that!" Julian protested. How could *she* think that?

"For a minute there, you did."

Julian stared out the window, blind to the view. He was only now coming to grips with how much his earlier suspicions had hurt her. How much *he* had hurt her.

"It'll probably be a blog post or an op-ed," she said, continuing as if she hadn't just gutted him. "I won't accept compensation."

Steam gushed out of the kettle with a hiss. He yanked the power cord out of the socket to quickly silence it. "I don't care about any of that."

"You may not, but everybody else does."

"Nina…" Since when did they care about what people thought? He did not recognize the people they'd become.

"One more thing," she said, hastily. "Katia thinks I should attend the Miami Film Festival. She said it would help if we present a united front. What do you think?"

None of his thoughts had anything to do with the film. He thought he'd messed up. The harm he'd caused was irreversible. He'd lost his lover and his friend, and

NADINE GONZALEZ **205**

nothing would ever make up for it. But Nina was waiting for an answer to her question. "I'd love to see you in Miami."

"All right," she said. "See you in Miami."

Three days later, Kat called with the news that Nina had published a blog post on the feminist website *Feminine-Plural*. For once she was too late. Nina had sent him a copy of the post the night before. That didn't stop him from spending his day at his desk, refreshing the website until the byline popped up in red print: *Her Name is Nina Taylor.*

> *Dear fans, followers and inquiring minds of all stripes:*
>
> *Thank you for your interest in the #1HOT KNIGHT affair.*
>
> *If you're not familiar with the scandal, I will get you up to speed. Last fall, my diary fell into the hands of an unscrupulous individual who ripped out a few pages and sold them to a gossip website. Those of you who've read the excerpt know more about my sex life than I'd be willing to share with my closest friends.*
>
> *The story begins in July. While on holiday in Miami, I met action movie star JL Knight. Our courtship got off to an unusual start. Day 1: We agreed to share a hotel suite. Day 2: He dived into a pool to save me. Day 3: We went on an excursion with his former landlady. Day 4: He kissed me in the moonlight.*
>
> *Don't take my word for it. There are photos documenting it all.*

*This love story should have remained a closed-bedroom-door romance. Instead, readers have been offered an explicit account of our most intimate encounter. My intention here is not to fill the few remaining cracks in your imagination. But since this is a story, and I'm a storyteller by nature, I would like to take this opportunity to flesh out the main characters, provide some context and backstory.*

*My name is Nina Taylor. The man who became my hero, friend, lover and creative partner is Julian Leroy Knight.*

*I am a writer. I've kept a diary since childhood. My journals have always been the guardian of my secrets. I've published a couple in the form of a memoir. However, that was a very different experience. I had control over the material and the process. Also, I had an editor to prune out the excess exclamation points and overabundance of clichés.*

*Julian is an actor, writer and filmmaker. He trusted me to read and revise the script he had spent years working on. We bonded over the written word. It is disheartening that words—my written words—caused so much havoc.*

*How this love story ends is none of your concern.*

*Over the next few weeks, I will be actively promoting* Midnight Sun *alongside my friend, director Julian Knight, and the countless other creative professionals who brought the film to life. Should we meet along the way, ask me about the creative process. I'd love to share. Ask me*

*about my private life and I'll have no problem
putting you in your place.*
　　*Thank you and be well.*

The following day, Julian met with Kat for lunch at
her favorite French bistro in West Hollywood. Kat was
her usual chatty self. Julian was sullen. Nina's words
pursued him, unsettled him. *Friend. Lover. Creative
partner.* How had he managed to lose all of that?

Kat was full of praise for Nina. "Mark my words. She
is now and for all time a feminist icon." She squeezed
a lemon into her iced tea. "Right up there with Rosa
Parks."

Julian raised his eyes from the menu. "Don't bring
Rosa Parks into this."

"Why aren't you happier?" Kat said. "She master-
fully rebranded you as an artist. JL Knight is dead. You
are now Julian Knight, a triple threat—actor, writer and
director."

"I don't care about that." Julian knew how insane that
sounded, because it was all he'd cared about up to this
point. "I betrayed her and let her down."

Kat reached for her glass of iced tea, knocking her
designer sunglasses clear off the table. Their waiter re-
trieved them, set a breadbasket on their table and took
their order. But Julian knew Kat well enough to know
when she was hiding something.

"Anything you want to tell me?" he asked once the
waiter had left.

Her blue gaze skidded away. Julian crossed his arms
and waited. Finally, she turned to him, composed. "It's
my fault you two split up. I called in the middle of the

night with all my theories and wouldn't drop it. What's wrong with me?"

"You were looking out for a friend," he said. "But I knew what I had with Nina. It was real, and I should never have been swayed."

"She loves you, you know."

Julian lowered his head and pinched the bridge of his nose, as if that simple gesture could keep him from falling apart. "But she hates me, too."

"That's to be expected," Kat said. "I'll say this—the woman I got a glimpse of in Miami last summer was not the woman I met with in New York. She tried to hide it, but she looked sad, dejected and disappointed as hell that you weren't traveling with me."

Sad? Dejected? He thought she'd be better off without him, but his better-off theory was proving to be bull. A guttural moan escaped him. "I want her back so badly. I don't want to go on like this. I don't think I can."

"Moaning to me about it won't get the job done, Knight."

He composed himself. "I need a strategy."

"Yeah, you do."

Julian grabbed a piece of crusty bread and tore it in half. It was going to take a heck of a lot of groveling and the mother of grand gestures to get Nina to consider forgiving him. "Would you mind helping me?"

She passed him the butter. "Thought you didn't want me to meddle."

"Does it make you uncomfortable? It's not exactly your job."

"Julian, we're friends!" she cried. "If I wanted to win someone back—or just get back at someone—I'd enlist you."

"And I'd say yes."

"Good," Kat said. "Now that we got that straightened out, let's strategize."

# Twenty-Four

*Miami Beach, Florida*

This was his night and she would play fair, but she reserved the right to be pissed.

Nina sprayed perfume on her wrists and slammed the delicate bottle on the marble vanity. One last glance in the bathroom mirror, and she was out the door.

During the ride from the hotel to the Fillmore theater, she repeated her mantra: *He's nothing to me. I'm over him.* It had been months since she'd laid eyes on Julian, but she was prepared. In the weeks leading up to the film festival, she'd built a sturdy emotional dam to keep her anger and resentment at bay. *I'm ready*, she thought. However, when the car pulled up to the red carpet and she spotted him standing there, elegant in a smoke-gray suit and sunglasses, she understood that she could never be ready.

There he was, her midnight sun.

He held open the car door. Nina looked up at his face, because she could never pass an opportunity to gaze at him. Her trained eye saw the man beneath the veneer. He looked fragile, as if he'd been shattered and pieced back together. His extended hand trembled slightly. She accepted it without hesitation. He squeezed tight, sending shivers racing up her bare arms, before helping her out of the car. Nina repeated her mantra, more frantically this time: *I'm over him. He's nothing to me.*

Under a hailstorm of flashing cameras, he stole a moment to whisper his thanks. "I can't tell you how much I appreciate this."

"I'm here to support the film," she whispered back. "We didn't work so hard for it to fail."

This movie was as much her own as anyone else's. She was proud to come out and support it. And with any creative project, she wanted it to be a smash hit.

"Whatever your reasons, I'm grateful you're here."

He pivoted and smiled for the remote pool of photographers sectioned off with velvet ropes. Nina was not the natural showman that Julian was proving to be. Her posture was stiff and her smile wobbly. She blamed her frayed nerves. It wasn't easy to face the cameras after all that she'd been through. Her weak knees had nothing to do with how close they were standing or his hand on the small of her back.

After what seemed like an eternity, Katia escorted her off the carpet. Bettina and Pierce had arrived, and it was time for her to yield her spot. "You did great. Now grab a glass a champagne and relax."

Valerie was waiting in the lobby. Nina's cousin was her plus-one for the event. Perceptive as always, Valerie hadn't missed a thing. "You two look amazing together, and, honestly, it's time for you to kiss and make up."

Nina kissed her cheek in greeting instead. "Shut up and show me to the concession stand."

With champagne, popcorn and gourmet snacks, they entered the packed auditorium. An usher escorted them to the front row, where Nina was reunited with Francisco and Grace, who appeared to be on a date.

*Midnight Sun* was a gorgeous film. Nina lost herself in the world that she'd had a hand in creating. From the opening scene with Bettina in a white bikini, floating on her back in that magnificent pool, to the end credits with Pierce driving into a citrus-hued sunset in a stolen white Camaro, frame for frame, the film was art in motion. The performances were as strong as the setting, and the audience rewarded the actors with a standing ovation. Julian was welcomed on stage for the director's Q&A to thunderous applause. He glowed with pride. Nina was bursting with love. She loved Francisco for having insisted he step up and direct. She loved the actors for their dedication. And she loved the audience for their warm reception.

Julian took a seat in a director's chair next to the evening's host, tall and lean and gorgeous. *He is nothing to me.*

Valerie nudged her in the ribs. "Relax! And quit glaring at the guy."

Nina could not relax. "Why does he look so good? It's distracting."

"How about you, #sexgoddess?" Valerie said, teasing. "Let me guess. Your trusty LBD was at the cleaners, so you grabbed a Grecian gown."

Nina had borrowed a play from her mother's book:

face your critics looking like a star. She'd headed straight
to Fifth Avenue and enlisted an in-house stylist at Saks
to help find the right dress: "I'm going to an event and
I'm not sure what kind of reception I'll get."

"Sounds like you're venturing into shark-infested
waters."

"Something like that. I need to look devastatingly
beautiful. Can you help me?"

"Darling, that's my expertise."

The gauzy one-shoulder dress she wore was the first
he'd put her in, but they'd kept coming back to it again
and again. She appreciated the way it hugged her figure,
but the pleats and folds made it easy to wear. To complete
the look, the stylist had insisted on gold accessories.
And to save a trip to a hair salon and stave off Miami's
humidity, Nina wore her hair in a long French braid.

"Ladies and gentlemen," the host said, "please welcome Julian L. Knight."

There was a fresh round of applause. Julian smiled
and waved, but his gaze swept the front row until his
eyes locked with hers. Nina's aggravation dissipated.
Briefly, they were alone in the packed auditorium. Nina
nodded her encouragement. All those nights they'd
stayed up working on the script and those long days on
set, she'd been with him almost from the start. She was
with him now. They might never ride off into the sunset
together, but she was on his side.

"Mr. Knight, you are better known as Thunder. From
action hero to movie director, that's quite a leap. How
did you go about it?"

"First I'd like to thank you for having me. I love
Miami Beach, and I'm happy to be back."

The audience cooed at his words. They loved him and

Nina loved them for loving him—although, to be sure, she still hated him.

"To answer your question, the story idea came to me a long time ago. I spent years working on it, but I could only take it so far. I had to wait for the right people to come into my life. People like your hometown hero, Francisco Cortes, whom I consider a mentor and father figure at this point." He paused for applause. Francisco twisted around in his chair and blew kisses to his fans. Grace looked proud and…for the first time ever, surly Grace Guzman looked happy. She also looked devastatingly chic in a black Versace dress, but that was classic Grace.

"I'm lucky enough to count my neighbor's nanny as one of my dearest friends," Julian continued. "At the right moment, she gave me the push I needed."

"Your neighbor's nanny!" the host exclaimed. "Are you comfortable sharing their name?"

"Absolutely. Rosie Parker." Julian scanned the audience. "Where are you, Rosie? Stand up and let the people see you."

A petite brunette stood from the second row and waved like Queen Elizabeth to great cheers. Nina dabbed away tears from the corners of her eyes. She'd never met Rosie, but had heard all about her. Some might be surprised that Julian would rather befriend the rich neighbor's nanny than the neighbor himself, but not Nina. He had such an open, generous heart. Not a pretentious bone in his hunky body.

"As someone who has followed your career in the press," the host said, "it sounds like you've grown a lot."

Julian nodded. "You could say that."

"Anyone else you'd like to thank publicly tonight?"

"Nina Taylor."

"Your cowriter?" the host asked, as if there were any doubt.

Nina had stiffened at the sound of her name. Should she stand and wave, too? Or could she slink under her chair? Soon, though, the theater went dark and the curtain rose. The movie screen lit up with a still image of her on the rooftop deck at Sand Castle, her linen shirtdress billowing in the breeze. It was the first photo he had taken of her. *I want you to see what I see.* That morning he had sent her a copy of the script; both their love affair and creative partnership had begun.

In the next photo, she was standing in the boat that Julian had chartered, staring at the turquoise sea. The sky was bursting with oranges and pinks, almost as if in celebration of a love they had not yet declared.

The photos that followed were candid shots taken by the cinematographer during production. She and Julian reading off the same script, walking around the set hand in hand, talking with the crew, laughing at jokes long forgotten, dancing at the wrap party.

When the lights flickered on, Julian stood alone on stage, looking down at her. Nina gripped the armrests, torn in two by terror and tenderness. He raised the microphone to his lips, and his smooth voice filled the theater. "You published your response, and now it's my turn."

*Oh, no...* She raised a hand to her forehead to shield her face. She did not want photographers capturing the moment she at long last came undone.

"Nina, you are my creative partner, my muse and my best friend. The night I lost you, I was more concerned with protecting my reputation than the woman I loved.

It pains me to admit it, but that's the awful truth. After you left, I didn't think you could ever forgive me, or that I even deserved forgiveness."

What was he doing? Hadn't he read her blog post? She'd been firm on keeping the public out of their affairs. He'd had every opportunity to speak with her. She did not want to have this conversation in a room full of strangers. "Julian, please," she said. "Don't do this."

"Goldie, let me say this one last thing."

He'd managed to turn a nickname that she despised into a sweet endearment. Damn him for weaponizing every tender memory! What was he trying to do? Rip her heart out of her chest?

"I betrayed you. And by staying away, I know I must have hurt you. All I wanted was to protect you—"

Someone heckled from deep within the audience. "Dump him, honey! He doesn't love you! This is all for show!"

Fueled by outrage, Nina jetted to her feet and faced the assembly. This was not the audience participation part of the show. "You don't know him! Mind your business!"

The response came lightning fast. "He made it our business!"

Nina couldn't argue against that. This grand romantic gesture wasn't worth their privacy. She swiveled around to take it up with Julian. Come to think of it, this did have all the trappings of a stunt. If he pulled a ring from his pocket and dropped to one knee, she would punch him in the face. Only Julian did not appear fazed by any of this. He laughed at the heckler. "I love this woman, and I don't care who knows."

Oh, God! That laugh! She remembered the first time

she'd heard it in the courtyard at Sand Castle, the day their eyes had met and she'd lost all good sense. This was her man. She loved him. There was no denying it.

"Just kiss and make up already!" Valerie cried. "This is killing me!"

Nina turned to confront her, but found her cousin, Grace and Francisco all beaming up at her encouragingly. She was reminded of what Grace had said the first night they'd talked: for some people, it takes a village.

She took one step toward the stage, one step toward Julian. His eyes were bright with emotion, and no force in the world could keep the words locked inside her. "I love you, Julian Knight. Okay? Happy? I love you! I don't want to live without you. Now, please stop trying to protect me from things. I hate it."

The assembly erupted in bravos and cheers. Julian dropped the microphone and smoothly leaped off the stage like the action star he absolutely was. He drew her into his arms and kissed her. They kissed as if a roomful of people were not watching, as if photographers weren't snapping photos like mad. He cupped her face and kissed her tenderly, lovingly, until Nina was out of breath and out of words to express her love. Then he released her, stepped away, pulled a ring out of his pocket and sank down on one knee.

Nina didn't hear the crowd gasp. All the world faded to black.

# Epilogue

"We're here on the red carpet with the *it* couple of the moment, Nina Taylor and Julian Knight. Welcome and congratulations on your engagement!"

"Thank you."

"Thanks."

"Julian, *Midnight Sun* is in the running for some of the night's top awards, including best director, best actress in a leading role and best original screenplay."

"Don't forget best cinematography."

"How could I forget? The film is so visually arresting! So, tell our viewers, how do you feel tonight?"

"Incredibly proud of the work and of the people who came together to make art. It is an awesome feeling."

"Nina Taylor, this is your first award season as a nominee. What is going through your mind?"

"I'm a little emotional. It was my mother's dream to walk the red carpet—and here I am!"

"Your mother was an actress."

"That's right. She's in my heart tonight, but it's wonderful to share billing with Julian. He thrust me into this. It's his job to see me through."

"Such a beautiful partnership! But speaking of partnerships, Bettina Ford credits you, Julian, for her breakthrough performance. What are your thoughts?"

"Bettina is a force of nature. She did not need any help from me."

"Nina, how do you plan to celebrate if you win?"

"As soon as the festivities are over, we fly back to Miami, where we plan to decompress. And by that I mean start working on the next project."

"What about wedding plans? Can you share anything about that?"

"Sorry. That's off-limits."

"No doubt! Well…best of luck you two, for tonight and forever."

*July 5. Julian Knight and Nina Taylor were wed last night in Miami Beach, Florida. The couple tied the knot at the hotel formerly known as Sand Castle. They exchanged vows poolside in front of fifty of their loved ones. Thereafter, the groom offered his bride the keys to the mansion as a wedding gift. They now have plenty of space to display the multiple awards won for their first collaborative effort,* Midnight Sun. —Vanities

\* \* \* \* \*

# COMING NEXT MONTH FROM

# HARLEQUIN
# DESIRE

## Available February 9, 2021

### #2785 BACK IN THE TEXAN'S BED
*Texas Cattleman's Club: Heir Apparent* • by Naima Simone
When Charlotte Jarrett returns to Royal, Texas, with a child, no one's more surprised than her ex-lover, oil heir Ross Edmond. Determined to claim his son, he entices her to move in with him. But can rekindled passion withstand the obstacles tearing them apart?

### #2786 THE HEIR
*Dynasties: Mesa Falls* • by Joanne Rock
To learn the truth about the orphaned boy she's raising, Nicole Cruz takes a job at Mesa Falls Ranch. Co-owner Desmond Pierce has his own suspicions and vows to provide for them. But he didn't expect the complication of a red-hot attraction to Nicole...

### #2787 SCANDALIZING THE CEO
*Clashing Birthrights* • by Yvonne Lindsay
Falsely accused of embezzlement, executive assistant Tami Wilson is forced into spying on her boss, CEO Keaton Richmond, to prove her innocence. But it isn't long until their professional relationship turns very personal. What happens when Keaton learns the truth...?

### #2788 ONE NIGHT WITH CINDERELLA
by Niobia Bryant
Shy housekeeper Monica Darby has always had feelings for handsome chef and heir to his family's fortune Gabe Cress. But one unexpected night of passion and a surprise inheritance change everything. With meddling families and painful pasts, will they find their happily-ever-after?

### #2789 SEDUCING HIS SECRET WIFE
*Redhawk Reunion* • by Robin Covington
A steamy tryst leads to a quickie Vegas wedding for notorious CEO playboy Justin Ling and his best friend's sister, Sarina Redhawk. Then, to please investors and their disapproving families, they continue a fake relationship. Are their feelings becoming all too real?

### #2790 TWICE THE TEMPTATION
*Red Dirt Royalty* • by Silver James
After a hurricane traps storm chaser Brittany Owens with tempting Cooper Tate, tension transforms into passion. But Cooper turns out to be her new boss! As their paths keep crossing, can she keep her promise to remain professional, especially when she learns she's pregnant—with twins?

---

**YOU CAN FIND MORE INFORMATION ON UPCOMING HARLEQUIN TITLES, FREE EXCERPTS AND MORE AT HARLEQUIN.COM.**

HDCNM0121

"Hopefully everyone will get home safe," she said.

Gabe took in her high cheekbones, the soft roundness of her jaw and the tilt of her chin. The scent of something subtle but sweet surrounded her. He forced his eyes away from her and cleared his throat. "Hopefully," he agreed as he poured a small amount of champagne into his flute.

"I'll leave you to celebrate," Monica said.

With a polite nod, Gabe took a sip of his drink and set the bottle at his feet, trying to ignore the reasons why he was so aware of her. Her scent. Her beauty. Even the gentle night winds shifting her hair back from her face. Distance was best. Over the past week he had fought to do just that to help his sudden awareness of her ebb. Ever since the veil to their desire had been removed, it had been hard to ignore.

She turned to leave, but moments later a yelp escaped her as her feet got twisted in the long length of her robe and sent her body careening toward him as she tripped.

Reacting swiftly, he reached to wrap his arm around her waist and brace her body up against his to prevent her fall. He let the hand holding his flute drop to his side. Their faces were just precious inches apart. When her eyes dropped to his mouth, he released a small gasp. His eyes scanned her face before locking with hers.

He knew just fractions of a second had passed, but right then, with her in his arms and their eyes locked, it felt like an eternity. He wondered what it felt like for her. Was her heart pounding? Her pulse sprinting? Was she aroused? Did she feel that pull of desire?

He did.

With a tiny lick of her lips that was nearly his undoing, Monica raised her chin and kissed him. It was soft and sweet. And an invitation.

"Monica?" he asked, heady with desire, but his voice deep and soft as he sought clarity.

"Kiss me," she whispered against his lips, hunger in her voice.

"Shit," Gabe swore before he gave in to the temptation of her and dipped his head to press his mouth down upon hers.

And it was just a second more before her lips and her body softened against him as she opened her mouth and welcomed him with a heated gasp that seemed to echo around them. The first touch of his tongue to hers sent a jolt through his body, and he clutched her closer to him as her hands snaked up his arms and then his shoulders before clutching the lapels of his tux in her fists. He assumed she was holding on while giving in to a passion that was irresistible.

Monica was lost in it all. Blissfully.

The taste and feel of his mouth were everything she ever imagined.

Ever dreamed of.

Ever longed for.

*Don't miss what happens next in*
One Night with Cinderella
*by nationally bestselling author Niobia Bryant!*

*Available February 2021 wherever*
*Harlequin Desire books and ebooks are sold.*

Harlequin.com